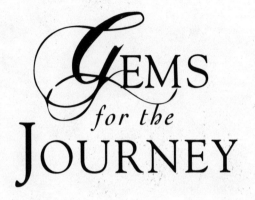

GEMS
for the
JOURNEY

GEMS
for the
JOURNEY

Vikki Johnson

NEW SPIRIT

BET☆
BOOKS

BET Publications, LLC
http://www.bet.com

NEW SPIRIT BOOKS are published by

BET Publications, LLC
c/o BET BOOKS
One BET Plaza
1900 W Place NE
Washington, DC 20018-1211

All Kensington Titles, Imprints, and Distributed Lines are available at special quantity discounts for bulk purchases for sales promotions, premiums, fundraising, and educational or institutional use. Special book excerpts or customized printings can also be created to fit specific needs. For details, write or phone the office of the Kensington Special Sales Manager: Attn. Special Sales Department, Kensington Publishing Corp., 850 Third Avenue, New York, NY 10022, Phone: 1-800-221-2647.

Library of Congress Card Catalogue Number: 2005922734
ISBN: 1-58314-657-1

First Printing: August 2005
10 9 8 7 6 5 4 3 2 1

Printed in the United States of America

This work is for all the women who thought wholeness was for everyone else. I share my journey so that you will be empowered to complete yours.

It is also dedicated to the women in my life whose journeys still inspire me, even though they have departed this life: Elizabeth "Sugarball" Snellings Williams and Marion "Mamoo" Smith Kennedy—my grandmothers.

Acknowledgments

This project is a prelude to my next work in progress, *Addicted to Counterfeit Love*. I need to mention this here because the following individuals have been instrumental in helping my journey to the place of *"perfect love"*:

To my Lord and Savior Jesus Christ: For drawing me closer to the "real thing" and for exposing me to the counterfeit first, so that I could tell others. You are the beginning, the center, and the end of my journey. Because of you I am excited about life.

To my first, earthly encounter with real love: My parents, Joyce Williams Kennedy and Art & Daisy Kennedy. ***Thank you for teaching me that nothing is impossible, and for loving me unconditionally!***

To the manifested heart of God in my life: Moriah Elizabeth — what I imagine for you is immeasurable. ***You are God's gift to me. Thank you for your smile, your unconditional love, and for sharing me with the world.***

To the best siblings a girl could have: Bruce, Artie, Jill, Janice, Lennard, Sharon, and all eighteen of my nieces and nephews. ***Thank you for being my place of refuge on this journey — even when you didn't know it.***

To the most loving, nurturing family in the whole, wide world: Williams, Kennedy, Waters, and Johnson clans — ***The legacy will never end.***

To my godchildren: Johntae, Brianna, Akiyyah, Abigail, and Lil Mike — ***You each add to my treasure.***

To my Spiritual Parents: Bishop Ralph and Elder Deborah Dennis — ***Ain't nothing like the real thang! Thank you for loving me as I journeyed to wholeness, and into my season of fruitfulness!*** To my Kingdom Worship Center family — ***Home is***

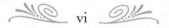

where the heart is. To Bishop Alfred and Co-Pastor Susie Owens—*Thank you for the solid foundation and for birthing me into the Body of Christ.*

To the "women of wisdom" God planted along my journey: Dr. Thelma Johnson; Gladys Gordon *(I thank God for USO)*; Gerri Butler; Doris Johnson; Pat Ross; Inez Bivins; Betty "Tee-Tah" Nelson; Ms. Roz *(it all started with the cheddar biscuits)*; Coach Marcia "Headlights" Pinder *(determination and hard work still equal success)*; Coach Sanya Tyler; Maye Jenkins; Sandra McDonald *(you added another dimension to my life)*; Velma McDowell; Aunt Dorothy M. Shaw *(God takes good notes)*; Mother Carrie Barnes—*Although I didn't come from your womb, you are my "other mothers" because God birthed me in your heart.*

To my "mentors" in ministry: Dr. Debyii Thomas; Wanda Frazier-Parker; Co-Pastor Katheran Mitchell; Pastor Doretha Best; Pastor Sonya Mixon; Dr. Eleanor Doom; Co-Pastor Renee Cole; Pastor Geraldine McInnis; Prophetess Arthurine Wilkinson; Tawanda Shepherd; Edna Owens; Lucy Dixon—*Each of you spoke life into my dry places and carried me until I could walk on my own. You each have taught me how to be a warrior and a woman. Thank you!*

If you understand the clue, you know it's you: "#4, sac—oh my"; "It started at the movie *Tootsie*"; "You bought my first bowling ball and taught me how to use it"; "Willow Grove"; A.W.O.L./LEV.; "Hello Love"; "Full Sail"; "You need to bring that in, Vikki"; "Winans/IHOP/almost trapped by the storm"; "You're my baby's godfather"; "VGR/3Fold/Dominion"; "Prestige/What's up, lady?"; "You've been there *since* HGC/Dathea"; "7D/Ballou/Nemo"; SPM; BabeBrice; "Seminole MS—when you found my daddy you found me"; I'm so glad you didn't wear off-white to the BET Awards; "Think Big Media." *Thank you for not taking advantage of the advantage, and for not allowing me to settle for the counterfeit experience. Good men still do exist!*

To the colors in my rainbow: Queen, Veda, Tia, Vivian, Qunea, Donise, Kecia, Portia, Twanda, Dee, Rosetta, Rose, Joanne, Pam, Kellie, Jacquie, Peggy, Paulette, Debra Heard, Shirley, K. Lyew, Aleathea, Annette, Artina, Sherri Jennings, Tiffany T-S, Marissa, Tori Dion, Lynnie, Yogi, Marketa, Felicia (my spec), (Mentees—Sher'ri, Rokia, Michelle, Kim Lee, Shelley, Deya, Kai, Tasha)—*Thank you for standing in the flames with me and loving me even when I smelled like ashes!*

To my childhood crew: Lisa, Helane, Shawn, Peaches (Debra), Twitty, Pop, Twalla, Taja, and Anthony—*We're evidence that friendships can last a lifetime.*

To Cheryl Jackson and the Heaven 1580AM family with love: This all started on February 14, 2002 . . . God's first hint of the future. *Thank you for the "urban inspiration."*

To the best attorney in the whole wide world: Debra Sims, Esq.—*You are one of the most "fearless" women I know. I still say you should have been a judge!*

To my BET family: When you do what you love, it's not work!

To Linda Gill: Thank you for "hearing my voice," and for the opportunity to share it with the world. Kicheko Driggins: *Thank you for the "push" to get it done and on your desk.* Selena Spencer: *I appreciate the "light" that you are—yup, I watch you.*

NABFEME (shout out to Johnnie, Sheila, & the Mid-Atlantic crew); Delta Sigma Theta Sorority, Inc. *(Orchidaceous 34)*; 14-A-85 *(God knew who to send and when. Thank you for letting me "do me")*; Delores, Tiffani, & the SGN; Theresa, Kelli (What's up, bootleg?), & *SiSDC*; Felicia & Sister2Sister; to the listeners of "I'm Every Woman" and the women who attend "Girl Talk" each quarter: *Each group makes up the DNA of my passion.*

And to you, the reader—The best is yet to come.

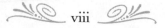

A Note of Encouragement
From a Mentor's Heart

*V*aluable, beautiful, captivating, precious are just a few of the ways in which we describe gems. They are deemed special because inherent in their structure is the ability to trap, transform, and transmit ordinary light into radiant, brilliant streams of light's energy. Gems impact not only the wearer, but also the beholder . . . oftentimes changing a blank stare into a beautiful smile. Too often, we forget that the gem does not start off as a gem, but as an ordinary mineral. Though the end of a gem is reflected in its exquisite beauty, the life of a gem is expressed through its resolve, its endurance, its tenacity in the face of the unbearable pressures and unending pains of its existence. It is not until the gem embraces its journey that the process begins.

Unfortunately, the gems have no way of knowing that their journey will be transforming, meaningful, even fulfilling. As God's chosen people, we can have an assurance that our journeys will not be in vain.

Elder Vikki Johnson is a Gem, in the truest sense of the word. One sees it in her life, her hope, her faith, her love. God uses her as a vessel reflecting Light and Life to those who, in their life journeys, cross her path as she answers destiny's call. I thank God that the Gem called Vikki took the time to share with others the gems that have brought her along the way. It is only natural, rather, supernatural, that she would open her

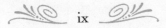

heart and allow God to trap, transform, and transmit His brilliance, His radiance, His sparkle through her.

Vikki's effort of faith will truly provide light and hope for your journey. These gems came from the journey of a sister who never gave up or gave in during the intense seasons of pressure and pain, confusion and chaos. Out of the storms, valleys, mountains, and pits, out of her love for God, for her natural and spiritual families, her kingdom friends, out of all of these things and more came these gems. They remind us that God *really* does care, that we *really* are special and that we *really* can make it!!!

Thank you, Elder, Sister, Girlfriend, Vikki!!! You've been a beautiful gem for my journey and in my life. Now, I celebrate with countless others as God will use you to be a **Gem for the Journeys** of His people all over His Kingdom and over this world. Shine, Sister, Shine!!! All my love . . .

Rev. Dr. Debyii S. Thomas
Assistant Pastor, Payne Memorial AME Church
Professor, Howard University School of Communications

Introduction
From a Sister's Heart

When I think of you, the reader, beginning your journey with my sister Vikki, I see myself as a stewardess urging you to buckle your seat belt, pay close attention, and prepare to meet your predestined life location full of new wisdom and divine understanding. What a way to enhance each day! Whenever I need insight, counsel, and guidance, I am very cautious of whom I trust to help me. It is critical for these select people to have battle scars proving to me they've been through hard places and know how to survive this thing called Life! It is mandatory that their knowledge come from a place of biblical application, humility, and compassion. Few people honestly fit this description. Many go through hard places, but often come out angry, bitter, and arrogant, still licking their wounds, wanting everyone to strengthen their "victim mentality." You must learn how to survive, heal, and then turn around to help others maneuver through their darkness. . . . That's where Vikki steps into your life. . . .

We met at a contemporary Asian cuisine restaurant in D.C. My friend Kellie Williams insisted that I meet Vikki, stating that we were similar creatures who would instantly connect. Kellie and I have become sisters over the years after walking with each other through some of those trying life moments when only genuine friends can help you; therefore, I trusted her belief that I would appreciate and respect this woman named Vikki Johnson. Meeting her face-to-face, I saw in her eyes a soul glow that said I am trusting, humble, and compassionate. Hours of conversation proved this to be true. Our words undressed our souls, exposed our kindred spirits, and revealed battle scars that had healed and stood as proof that victory can eradicate victim living! From that point on she was a Sister.

My life set sail on stormy waters from birth—I was born with birth "defects" that required orthopedic surgery from then until seventeen years of age. Raised by a successful widow due to my father's unfortunate death from cancer, I forced my three fingers to learn how to play the harp and piano. My family relocated to Virginia from California when I was in the eighth grade. I was the first black to graduate from a prestigious prep school, which taught me the art of people not having to like you, but always needing to respect you. I then attended Howard University, and beyond the "black experience at the Mecca," I failed to make my medical career dream a reality because I was called into the ministry. I have since spent my life dedicated to helping people dumped on the trash piles of life overcome rejection and defeat.

Women like Vikki may not have my exact story, but they have pushed past enough drama to play on the silver screen. Thus you receive words of strengthening encouragement from a woman who has battled mentally, emotionally, spiritually, physically, and relationally. *Gems* is a three-course meal that is delectable, delightful, and delicious! The chef serves you like you are at a royal party, but with the intimacy of a private dinner setting. Trust me—this is coming from a Sister's Heart that knows you can eat here and be satisfied. There is room at the table, and we invite you to be a guest. I represent a host of sisters who trust Vikki to be personable, integral, and kindhearted. So dig in daily and find out why we call her our sister! Kellie . . . thank you for sharing this Gem of a sister with me!

Follow Peace and Be Encouraged,

Rev. Theresa McFaddin, Sisters Inspiring Sisters
www.HarvestWords.com

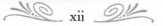

Foreword
From a Father's Heart

Inside of every woman is a little girl whose identity was either strengthened or shattered by her father. Her self-confidence was either built up or broken by the one man she felt connected to. Inherent in every woman is the need for the protection of a man who loves her with the "pure love" of God. Frequently, men abuse that access and thus leave broken trust, scattered hearts, and a fragmented capacity to live meaningful lives.

Quite often, women continue to develop physically, while experiencing retarded growth emotionally, mentally, and spiritually. Consequently, many women believe that where they are is all there is. This journey called life is full of ups and downs, triumphs and trials, victories and defeats that all lead to a place called destiny, if you embrace the process of the journey.

In Gems for the Journey my daughter gives an explicit and clear picture of how capable God is of preserving each of us for purpose. When you get a revelation or "picture" of who God created you to be, you are then released to live life in a way you have never known before . . . abundantly and victoriously.

If you are reading this book, it is evidence that you have been hand-picked by God to make an impact that will never be forgotten. Don't take this opportunity lightly. This is your time to expose who you really are and to manifest what you were born to do. If not now, then when? When you really come to understand the power that is available to you to efficiently and effectively manage your life, you will no longer succumb to the "it just happened moments" orchestrated by adversity, frustration, and unresolved pain. I challenge you to make a commitment to the "process of becoming whole" — engaging whatever it takes so that you can become ALL that you were created to be.

Of course, the plight of the woman is not necessarily an act of God. There is a subjective element in the form of a virulent bias embedded in commercial, legal, and social sectors that reduces the life chances of women, particularly those of African descent. The only way such a plight can be successfully overcome and maintained, is via the one subjective element each woman possesses from her creator — the choice of renewal. Purpose is locked into the exercising of this choice. Life is a perpetual series of interrogatories, until that ultimate choice is made. Only the Creator can make clear, through redefinition and refining, purpose that leads to abundant living. Only the new creation and the renewed mind can optimize one's potential. All else is less than "absolute" fulfillment.

The idea of the female challenge in life and living is not a recent theme. Yet, Vikki has been gifted by her own life's experiences to share awesome insights that release victory and resist defeat. May you be strengthened as you read *Gems for the Journey*. Have a great trip!

Bishop Ralph Dennis
Vikki's (Spiritual) Father
Senior Pastor, Kingdom Worship Center

Before The Journey Begins
... *The Commencement*

*L*et me share with you a few things. Every journey is different. Along the way each of us learns valuable "life lessons" that help us become whom God intended. Every encounter of pain peels away a layer of the "stuff" that hides our true selves. As you embark upon this journey, know that it will challenge you to face some things that you have been avoiding. It will provoke you to look in the mirror and see what you have been covering up. It will push you out of the familiar and into the unknown. Every mind, body, and spirit gem includes space for you to take notes—notes to God, notes to self, notes to others who may share your route.

God desires that you prosper and be in health, even as your soul prospers. However, "God prosperity" is not one-dimensional, but multifaceted. God is concerned about your spiritual, mental, emotional, physical, and relational health. We cannot have total victory in one area without total victory in all areas. These gems are to give you a "jump start" to holistic living. There is the commencement, your official start; the checkup, your midpoint evaluation; and the continuation to the next level of living. The journey does not end; it just begins again in a new place.

You, the reader, are my inspiration. I did not endure and survive my journey to this point just for me. I went through it to help you get through yours. You are going through your

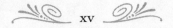

journey to help someone else. It's not about you at all. Every step of your journey is so that the glory in you can come out and light the way for those whom you are being empowered to impact.

A journey is a *"trip from one place to another."* You are on your way from "never again" and on your way to "never before." All you need is courage, honesty, and expectation of "better." Every step forward moves you closer to your destination of wholeness. Let's get started because we have work to do. . . . Yes, **"WE"** have work to do.

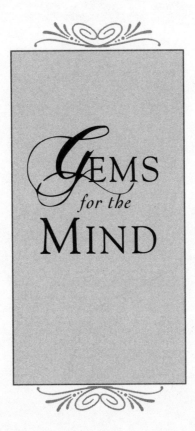

GEMS
for the
MIND

1 *Today's Gem*

Are you living by default or are you living by God's design for your life? If you are living by default, it means you just let life happen. If you are living by God's design, it means you live a life of purpose on purpose every day. You approach each day knowing that your steps are ordered by God. Living by design means you and God plan the day together. Living by default is living beneath your privilege, Sis. When you live by default, your life is also blessed by default. However, when you live by design, your life is full of good things—for the Bible declares in **Psalm 84:11,** "No good thing will He withhold from you if you walk uprightly before Him."

Journey Note

2 Today's Gem

In reality, there's a price to pay for living out the fantasy. Girl, keep it real! Make sure you can live with the consequences of your choice. **Deuteronomy 30:19** says, "I call heaven and earth as witnesses today against you, that I have set before you life and death, blessing and cursing; therefore choose life, that both you and your descendents may live." Don't mistake God's silence for God's approval. Keep it real. If you face the truth, God can reconcile you to the truth. Don't be deceived, God is not mocked—whatever you sow, you will surely reap. Why? Because time has a big mouth—eventually, time tells everything.

Journey Note

3   *Today's Gem*

Follow-through is the way to breakthrough! You cannot circumvent the process of God to get to the promise. Anything worth having is worth fighting for. Cutting corners is a sign of immaturity, impatience, and inconsistency. Author Albert Grey says, "The common denominator of all success lies in forming the habit of doing things that people who fail don't like to do." Successful people have learned to do what does not come naturally. They confront fear, discomfort, and distractions and act in spite of them. Discipline to be successful is only acquired through practice.

Journey Note

4   *Today's Gem*

Now is the time to get your life in order! How do you proceed? You proceed by committing every area of your life to the obedience of God's Word. Then you must commit to beginning each day with God by reading His Word, talking to God, and sitting quietly waiting for Him to talk back to you. Ladies, get your finances in order by becoming a good steward of what God has released to you. Do you really need another pair of shoes? The next time you're tempted to spend money, ask yourself: *Do I really have to have it?* God wants you to live in overflow—but first you must prepare for it!

Journey Note

5 *Today's Gem*

What you used to do and who people knew you as doesn't matter anymore. In spite of your mistakes, in spite of your mess-ups, in spite of your past and maybe your present misery, God's purpose in your life still stands. God is great enough to give you a new start even when others have given up on you! Sis, you're not that person anymore. When you get down to the bottom line—your history may be recorded; folks may choose to remember and try to hold it against you—but God won't even refer to it when it's time to fulfill your destiny. Live as unto the Lord!

Journey Note

6 *Today's Gem*

Too many people grow older without growing up and maturing. Growth ALWAYS begins with a decision. You must want to grow, decide to grow, make an effort to grow, and persist in growing. Nothing shapes your life more than the commitments you make. They either develop you or destroy you, but either way they define you. Every choice you make has consequences, so choose wisely. Christ-likeness is the result of making Christ-like choices, then depending on Him to help you fulfill those choices. **Ephesians 4:15** declares that God wants us to grow up like Christ in everything. If you haven't asked yourself in the past, then consider this question the next time you make a decision: WHAT WOULD JESUS DO?

Journey Note

7   *Today's Gem*

Are you still aligned with what was? Are you stuck waiting for what will be? If you find yourself focused on the past or the future, you are missing the precious gift of NOW! Now is a wonderful place to be! When tough times come, we have a tendency to lower our expectations and end up settling for less than God wants us to have. In order to appreciate NOW, we must live by faith. Now faith is the substance of things hoped for, the evidence of things not seen. By remaining attached to what's familiar and what's always worked, we seriously limit what God can do for us. God is not predictable. God is not enhanced by your strength or limited by your weaknesses. There's more He wants to do through you than what you've experienced this far. It can begin right now!

Journey Note

8 *Today's Gem*

True deliverance is the abolishment or destruction of your affliction! Once you commit in your mind to allow God to deal with your stuff, you must remove yourself from all the things that facilitated the pain, the habit, the issue, while the power of God heals you and makes you whole. It's called recovery. Recovery takes time. What if you can't remove yourself? Then, Sis, hide yourself in the secret place of His presence— your environment might not change, but I guarantee that you will. The more time passes, the easier it becomes to walk out and embrace the new you. God wants to heal you. God can heal you—the question is: Do you really want Him to do so?

Journey Note

9   *Today's Gem*

This is your time to impact the world. Mediocrity is normal and most prevalent. Excellence is rare and hard to find. Expand your possibilities! Get out of your neighborhood and do something different. Better is coming your way! You can have so much more. First, you must want more. God has put you in the location where you are to make a difference. Invest in God's purpose for your life. God refreshes us and then equips us to be a resource to others. Who is better because you're there? Listen, ladies, God is never limited by our limitations. In fact, our greatest weakness can become our greatest weapon if we allow it to point us toward God. Unwrap yourself and give your all to God. You are a masterpiece waiting to be displayed!

Journey Note

10 *Today's Gem*

A rainbow would be boring if it consisted of only one color. Likewise, your life can be boring if you only have one way, one idea, one routine, one dream, one aspiration, or one philosophy. God is in each of us, and therefore, in us is diversity, creativity, trailblazing and pioneering ability, courage, intellect, and wisdom to do what has never been done before. Sis, with Christ as the center of your life—live in many different directions; enjoy new opportunities, and maximize every moment given to you. There's only one of you—and you only get one life to live.

Journey Note

11 *Today's Gem*

Before you can move into the new, you must tear down and destroy the old. God is faithful, God is love, God is our banner and shield—and God is also jealous. He will not share your devotion. He will not share your heart. He will not force you to love Him, because He draws you with loving-kindness if you're paying attention. Resist the temptation to stay like you are. **Psalm 34:10** says those who seek the Lord shall not lack any good thing. God made a promise to you in **Exodus 34:10.** God said to stop and take note of the fact that He's given you a promise. The promise is if you obey Him, He will do exploits in your life and people will know you belong to Him. It is an awesome thing that He will do with you. God is waiting for you in the unknown so you can live like you've never imagined.

Journey Note

12 *Today's Gem*

How do you define success? Is it measured by security or is it measured by fulfillment? I submit to you that success is measured by both. Security is defined as knowing that your job is your resource and that God is your source. Fulfillment is defined as knowing that you have made an impact that is eternal and God gets all the glory. In essence, when you find a job you love, you're content to stay forever. Don't do what you do for the money, recognition, prestige, or satisfaction. Do what you do because you know in your heart it's the reason you were born. Wherever God gives vision, He makes provision. So again I ask—how do you define success?

Journey Note

13 *Today's Gem*

It's time to change! Don't delay your response to what you know God is requiring you to do. Delay breeds missed opportunities, which produce nothing but frustration. Sis, some of us have been in neutral for too long. Make a decision and let God work out the details. The only way to get out of neutral is to SHIFT! Shift your thinking in the direction of the Lord. Shift your emotions in the direction of His presence so He can settle your heart with joy. Shift your spirit to a place of hunger and thirst for righteousness so you can be filled. Everything must change—nothing stays the same. On your mark, get set, CHANGE.

Journey Note

14 *Today's Gem*

The power of decision gives you the capacity to get past any excuse not to change any and every part of your life in an instant. Halfhearted wanting or desire does not propel us forward. In order to manifest change, we must embrace focus plus intention (which is aiming with a plan). Make a decision to live a resurrected life. Make space in your life for what's important to you. Make a decision right now to become proactive instead of reactive. Proactive people prepare for the future while effectively managing now. Reactive people focus on fixing yesterday and mismanaging their now. The choice is yours. All you have to do is make a decision.

Journey Note

15 *Today's Gem*

When constant fear, pessimism, and paranoia become your mind-set, you have failed to paint your life with the promises of God. If you always see the glass as half empty, you are shortchanging your life with doubt and unbelief. If God is your everything, then your life is full and you are content. If your life is not full and you are not content, it follows then that God has not yet become what you say He is in your life. Why should people come to church with you or even want to be around you to discover a God who keeps you depressed and negative all the time? Sis, what does your life say about your Savior? What do your words say about your Lord? Think about it—what does Jesus look like, think like, when people encounter you?

Journey Note

16 Today's Gem

Many of us use church as a trampoline out of our emotional and psychological valleys every week. We start from the bottom every Sunday morning, and consequently, church becomes a routine that never seems to satisfy. We expect the worship experience to lift us out of the low place we settle into—sometimes before we leave the parking lot. Thus, it's hard for us to comprehend that life can be lived in the high places ordained. Truth is, you can live in the high places of God when you expect an encounter with God on Sunday. This encounter is not just for an emotional release—it's to give you an exciting revelation of who you are in Him. **Habukkuk 3:19** says "the Lord God is my strength, and He will make my feet like hinds' feet, and He will make me to walk upon mine high places." Once God lifts you, keep going up.

Journey Note

17   *Today's Gem*

You were not an accident. God made you so that He could love you. You are the object of God's love and affection. Your life has profound meaning and you were created to have profound impact. There is no one else like you. Your identity comes from God. Who you are is not based on what you do. God says that you belong to Him. That means when you no longer do what you do, you'll still be who you are to God: the apple of God's eye!

Journey Note

18 *Today's Gem*

Take a step. Now take another step. Yes, one step at a time. The worst thing you can do when you're afraid is nothing. Sitting around hoping things will change will leave you paralyzed with fear. Sis, you always have a choice. Taking just one step or making just one move robs fear of its power in your life. Which direction should you move? I'm glad you asked—take a step toward God and it will lead you to new levels of insight, understanding, and options. You always have a choice.

Journey Note

19 *Today's Gem*

Who are you when no one is looking? Who are you when everyone is looking? Do you know and/or are you familiar with yourself? I'm talking about who you really are, not who you want to be. Today, make a commitment not to allow your environment to alter your identity. Find your identity in Christ and through Christ for He is able to empower you to be whom He created you to be. You are destined for greatness and are on your way the moment you release the facades, the roles you play, and the fears that cause you to compromise. Come out of hiding and live the life God has prepared for you.

Journey Note

20 Today's Gem

You can begin again. As long as you have life, you have hope. It's never too late to begin again. First, however, you need to confront the reasons why you are in the place you're in. Be honest with yourself. Examine your mistakes and bad choices and learn the lesson. Separate what makes sense and what is nonsense. Medicine for physical ailments does not taste good but it helps. Spiritual medicine for the process of healing does not feel good initially but it works. Let's get busy and uncover our secret pain so we don't sabotage or destroy possibilities that ARE coming. Your story is not over, Sis— just turn the page.

Journey Note

21  Today's Gem

What are you holding on to that God has asked you to release? Who has a hold on your present because they were a part of your past? Girl, listen. You cannot move forward and continue to reach back at the same time. This posture or position renders your present useless because you're stuck. Stuck is a bad place to be because life just passes you by. Time waits for no one, but gives everyone a chance. What are you going to do with the next opportunity that requests for you to grow? What are you afraid of? God was in your yesterday; He's with you today; and He'll be waiting in your tomorrow. Hey, Sis— hold out for healing. Don't try to reattach yourself in order to stop the pain. Walk with God one day at a time. He will soothe and eventually heal your ragged edges and emotions. Hold out for wholeness—it takes time. You may have to cry some more, and that's okay. The Bible tells us that weeping may endure for a night, but joy comes in the morning. To get to the morning you must endure the midnight of the day before. The closer you draw to God, the more He fills your empty, barren places. The longer you dwell in His presence, the more He overshadows you with His comfort. In **Matthew 11:28,** Jesus invites you to "come to me, all you who labor and are heavy laden, and I will give you rest." Construct a throne of praise in your heart and the miracle you seek will manifest. Don't look far—the miracle is ALREADY in you!

Journey Note

22 Today's Gem

From an acorn to an oak tree . . . what an incredible journey. God's intention when He made the acorn was the oak tree. When you were born, His intention for you was the measure of the fullness of the stature of Christ. God never intended for you to get stuck in your mistakes. Acorns survive process and you can, too. We must continue to die to old habits, old thought patterns, and old comfort zones. In order to reach our potential, we must endure many "letting go of" experiences. However, when you look at the oak tree, you don't even think of the acorn. Likewise, the more you perceive God's purpose for your life, the less you will feel the pain of letting go.

Journey Note

23   *Today's Gem*

    Get up and do something. Today is your day to do something different. Girl, you have the authority and the right to walk by faith and not fear. Fear paralyzes you—faith causes you to move. Fear restricts you—faith increases you. Fear makes you worry—faith provokes you to worship. Fear says God is taking too long—faith reminds you that He is always there when you need Him. Fear torments you to give up—faith empowers you with sufficient grace to do anything you can see in your mind. Start now and only focus on today. Do the best you can and at the end of your ability is God's opportunity.

Journey Note

24   *Today's Gem*

Live each day to the fullest. Stop living life in pieces. A piece of you is in yesterday; a piece of you is in tomorrow; and at the same time, you're wasting God's precious gift of today. Author Jim Elliott once wrote, "Don't let your longings, anxiety, and loneliness destroy your appetite for living." Self-pity is a deadly thing with power to destroy you. **Matthew 6:34** declares, "Sufficient for EACH day is its own trouble." But guess what, Sista Girl? His grace is sufficient, too!

Journey Note

25 *Today's Gem*

Don't get stuck in that place of indecision. Make a choice today and trust God. Stop worrying about what you have no control over and trust God! Yes, the short-term result of your choice may be painful. But, Sis, fear not. God will give you grace to endure and courage to hold your ground. You've put this off long enough. Listen, counterfeit peace is worse than no peace at all because you live in fear knowing that at any moment it could change. Whoever you are today, do what you need today — do what you need and know to do. Let God work out the details. He is there — on the other side of that choice — waiting to pick up the broken pieces! Trust God!

Journey Note

26 *Today's Gem*

What do you do, Sis, with feelings of loneliness, longing, insecurity, anger, bitterness, unforgiveness, and jealousy? You give it to Jesus. In the spirit of your mind, make a determination to give your issue or issues to Him. Why? It's material for sacrifice. Elizabeth Elliott, noted author and speaker, said, "The transformation into something He can use for the good of others takes place only when the offering is put in His hands." Give it to Jesus—you can't do anything with it. Offer it to our Father—He's waiting to transform your pain into power that manifests purpose!

Journey Note

27 Today's Gem

What do you do when you don't know what to do? **Psalm 46:10** says, Be still, Shhhhhh! Know, understand, and recognize that He is God! Know that the Lord is with you. Be not afraid or dismayed at what appears to be larger than life—this battle is not yours, it's the Lord's. Trials, trauma, and transition come to push us into the next level of freedom. Listen, Sis, frustration, discouragement, and impatience come in like a flood—JUST before your breakthrough! Friend, the last thing God said is sufficient until He speaks again. Take your position—stand still. You shall not need to fight this one!

Journey Note

28 *Today's Gem*

Are you a silent sufferer? Are you going through turmoil that only you and God know about? Is your heart bleeding from pain too much for you to bear? Well, Sis, I want to remind you that the word of God is full of prescriptions that will set you free—if you would only follow instructions. In times like these, David said in **Psalm 142** the Lord was his refuge. **Psalm 46:1** declares that "God is our refuge and strength, a very present and well proven help in troubled times." **Psalm 61** tells us to "cry out to God—when your heart is overwhelmed and fainting, lead me to the rock that is higher than I—for the Lord is a shelter and refuge." You've tried everything and everybody else—now try God. He's waiting with open arms.

Journey Note

29   *Today's Gem*

"STUFF HAPPENS"! So many women are still bound by "STUFF" that has happened in their lives. Stuff like drugs, sex, abortion, betrayal, abuse, divorce, single parenting, and rape, to name a few. God knows about your stuff and He wants you to know that He has made provision for the "stuff" that has happened to you. **Hebrews 4:15–16** says, "we have not a high priest who cannot understand and sympathize with us, but that we can fearlessly draw near to the throne of grace for help in our time of need." Jesus has felt the pain of your stuff. Today, He wants you to know His grace is sufficient— even for your stuff.

Journey Note

30   *Today's Gem*

There are two enemies of today. Regret from yesterday and fear of tomorrow. But the Bible tells us in **Philippians 3:13** to "forget what lies behind and press forward to what's waiting for you." Live each day to the fullest. Maximize every single moment. Take the opportunity to create memories whenever and wherever you can. Yesterday is gone forever and tomorrow may never come. But you do have today. What a wonderful gift today is. Shoulda, woulda, coulda, and what ifs rob you of NOW! There is power in now. Today, God wants you to embrace His image of you. When you begin to view life from His perspective, the insignificant becomes significant.

Journey Note

31 _Today's Gem_

Why are you worried about tomorrow? **Matthew 6:34** says, "Therefore, do not worry about tomorrow, for tomorrow will worry about its own things. Sufficient for each day is its own trouble." Worrying about tomorrow affects your relationship with God today. Worry is an affliction based on "what if"! What if the money doesn't come? What if I never get married? What if my children never get off drugs? What if God doesn't heal me? What if I get a pink slip at work? What if, what if, what if! **Philippians 4:6–7** says, "Be anxious for nothing, but in everything by prayer and supplication with thanksgiving let your requests be made known to God." If you do that, God has guaranteed that "His peace will surpass your worry and guard your heart and mind through Jesus Christ."

Journey Note

32 _Today's Gem_

Don't get complacent in the wrong place just because God is allowing you to be stimulated. There's a difference between being stimulated and being sustained. God has more for you than where you are. You can change if you REALLY want to. **Proverbs 16:9** tells us that "we can count on God to direct our steps." Stop looking for someone else to bring you happiness, success, and fulfillment. **Galatians 6:4–5** tells us, "Let each one examine his work and then he will have rejoicing in himself alone, and not in another. For each one shall bear his own load." Get over yourself and get busy on God's agenda for your life—you can change if you really want to.

Journey Note

33   *Today's Gem*

There is nothing like the real thing. If you've ever experienced anything counterfeit, then you'll agree—ain't nothing like the real thing. It's the same way in God. A superficial or surface pursuit of God leaves us vulnerable to paranoid loneliness, cheap sex that makes us feel empty, and an accumulation of loads of mental and emotional garbage, and eventually a detachment takes place that causes you to view everyone as a rival. Sis, what kind of living is that? Christ-filled living is not just an idea in your head or a sentiment in your heart. Read **Galatians 5:22–33** today. Strive to manifest Christ in every area of your life.

Journey Note

34 Today's Gem

Don't quit! It's an easy choice when you are hardest hit—but this unknown author said rest if you must, but don't you quit. It's the silver lining on the clouds of doubt; success is failure turned inside out. John Maxwell, noted author and speaker, said, "The difference between average people and achieving people is their perception of failure and their response to it." Author John Hubbard wrote: "There is no failure except in no longer trying." **Proverbs 24:16** says, "For a righteous man falls seven times and rises again." **Galatians 6:9**: "Be not weary in well doing, for in due time and at the appointed season, you shall reap and receive if you don't relax your courage and faint." When you want to smile but you have to cry, step back, rest in God, relax a bit. Girl, you are God's woman, and we DON'T QUIT!

Journey Note

35   *Today's Gem*

Philippians is a prescription for peace for the believer. **Chapter 1:6** tells us to be confident—because if God started it, He will finish it. **Chapter 3:13–14** admonishes us to forget what's behind and press forward. **Chapter 4:6** challenges us to stop worrying and allow God's peace to consume us so that our hearts and minds are protected. **Chapter 4:13** empowers every woman listening and reading that through Christ who strengthens you, you can do all things. **Chapter 4:8–9** tells us how—by thinking about what's true, noble, just, pure, lovely, and of a good report. Once you reach this place of peace, **Chapter 4:19** promises us, "And my God shall supply all your need according to His riches in glory by Christ Jesus." Rest, God's got your back!

Journey Note

36   *Today's Gem*

The word of the Lord for you today is *Up!* You are in a season of up. Hold your head up. You are on your way up. Don't you dare give up. It's time to make your mind up. Clean your house up. From the muck and mire God said get up. You've been down long enough. Today, woman, God calls you forth to facilitate the manifestation of a mighty victory—victory in your life and victory in the life of all who are attached to you. You are not warring to win—you are warring to manifest the victory that's already been won. **Judges 4:14:** "And Deborah said to Barak, Up! For this is the day when the Lord has given Sisera into your hand!" In other words, today is your day of freedom!

Journey Note

37   *Today's Gem*

Change is a choice. It's about making decisions. No matter how difficult, no matter how impossible it appears to be, remember, with God nothing shall be impossible. God is the God of all flesh and in Him we live, move, and have our being. In Him, change is constant because we decrease as He increases in us. It's called metamorphosis. It's called becoming "in time" who we already are "in eternity." It's called being renewed in the spirit of your mind so that you can be renewed in every other area of your life, too.

Journey Note

38 *Today's Gem*

God won't tell you what you don't need to know. Further, He won't do what He's already told you to do. **Proverbs 3:5** says, "Trust in the Lord with all thine heart; and lean not unto thine own understanding." Sis, when you put something in God's hands and say you're going to trust Him with it, don't take it back because you don't like the way He's handling it, or the length of time He's taking to deal with it. We don't like unanswered questions but they are tools God uses to train us in trusting Him. When you don't have the answer, you can either (1) worry, (2) try to figure it out yourself (which is another form of worry, by the way), or (3) TRUST GOD!

Journey Note

39 Today's Gem

Years ago Bobby McFerrin released a single admonishing the world "Don't Worry, Be Happy." When you think about it, God told us the same thing in **Philippians 4:6–7.** "Be anxious for nothing, but in everything by prayer and supplication, with thanksgiving, let your requests be made known to God." Verse 7 continues, "and the peace of God, which surpasses all understanding, will guard your hearts and minds through Jesus Christ." Worry only leads to compromise. Compromise makes you vulnerable to temptation. Temptation opens the door to sin. Sis, take your burdens to Abba Father (Daddy) and leave them there.

Journey Note

40 *Today's Gem*

It's not money that's evil. It's the love of money that causes destruction. **1 Timothy 6:9–10** says, "But those who crave to be rich fall into temptation and a snare and into many foolish, useless, godless, and hurtful desires that plunge men into ruin and destruction. For the love of money is the root of all evil." When you chase money, greed, arrogance, and lust take over your life. You'll do anything to anybody to make a dollar. When you find your security in Christ, you can rest in the fact that your money, your blessings, your promises, your favor, and your wealth are looking for you—to overtake you.

Journey Note

41 Today's Gem

Women were created with power. But often, too many women abuse this power because they don't understand the purpose of this power. Abuse is inevitable when purpose is not understood and/or is ignored. Purpose is to be understood and embraced so that power can be released. Women were given this power to have dominion and effect positive change. Far too many of us use this power to manipulate for personal gain. Come out from behind the veil of hurt, pain, shame, abuse, apathy, cynicism, doubt, unbelief, disappointment, and disillusionment. God has power waiting for you that needs to flow through a pure heart, a pure mind, and a pure soul. Seek purity and you'll find power untold.

Journey Note

42 *Today's Gem*

Every now and then we need to calibrate our surroundings. In other words, check your location and make the necessary adjustments. Take the precious time to look back over your life and see where you were; examine the progress of now; and expect in, hope for, and rest in the promises of your future. Don't focus on or get so distracted by your weaknesses, flaws, and vulnerabilities that you forget to expand on your strengths to create an incredible life. Don't just undo what's wrong, but build on what's right. Today is your day to resurrect a dream— and ascend to your destiny.

Journey Note

43 *Today's Gem*

It's really worth it! Give up what you're holding on to so God can give you what He has for you. Unfortunately, some of us would rather do well on the wrong road than struggle and stumble on the right road. What are you waiting for? Look for God in the ordinary to get the extraordinary. Hold firmly to hope because it keeps you focused. Keep the main thing the important thing so you can get to the right thing for your life. With God, ALL things are possible.

Journey Note

44 *Today's Gem*

Is there a war going on in your mind? Yes, you've got a great job, a nice car, and a fabulous shape, BUT you're suicidal. Or maybe you're tired of pretending that your marriage is wonderful and your children are happy. You are really tired of the facade and just can't take it anymore. Snap, crackle, and you were about to pop—BUT GOD! God today says come unto me all ye that labor and are heavily laden—I will give you rest. God says His yoke is easy and His burden is light. God says His grace is sufficient for you, so cast your care upon Him for He cares for you. Bring that lie you are living to the truth of God's love—He wants to make it like it's supposed to be.

Journey Note

45 Today's Gem

When we step over boundaries that God sets in place, we set ourselves up for disappointment, disaster, disorder, and disarray. The order of God is for women to be feminine and for men to be masculine. Ladies, let the man be the man. Too often, we assist the men in our lives to our own detriment. Ladies, if you are single, the Lord will shoulder your load and make up the difference. If you are married, release your husband to the tutoring of the Lord to fulfill his role as the priest of your home. Stop rescuing him! Stop being consumed by unrealistic expectations. Let him be what God designed him to be. Cast your care upon the Lord for He cares for you. God does not need your help in manifesting fruitfulness in his life. He only asks for your agreement with the plan He has already laid out. Girl, God is up to something and He is dealing with your man on your behalf!

Journey Note

46 *Today's Gem*

Happiness is a choice. Not something based on other people's actions. Too often, our unmet needs are based on illusions, fantasies, and insecurities that we have yet to release to God. A lot of women have a misguided definition of love. To these women, love is cards, flowers, sex, emotional neediness, and unrealistic expectations of others. This is not God's intended expression of love. Real love goes much deeper than this. Real love is unconditional, unchanging, and understanding. Real love is a commitment, a choice, and a covenant. Real love is an intangible miracle that is sometimes expressed in tangible ways. Real love stays when others go away. To ensure that you are positioned to receive love the way God intended, make sure you are responding to God and not reacting to people!

Journey Note

47 *Today's Gem*

Denial is a dangerous state of mind to be in. Some women prefer living a lie because in their mind, it's easier than facing the truth. But you must come face-to-face with the truth before the truth can set you free. Hiding only prolongs the pain, agony, frustration, and deceit that God wants to deliver you from. Yes, light exposes and it also causes the darkness to disappear. Come on out, girl, and walk in the light. Walk into the presence of the Lord so you can experience life like never before. The light of God's love will cause the darkness of your denial to go away!

Journey Note

48   *Today's Gem*

Come into today with a clean slate. Activate the gift of good-bye. Your destiny was never tied to anything you weren't born with or to anyone that has ever left you. If you needed it, you would still have it. If you needed them, they would still be around. God knows what you have left and He knows it's enough. God knows who is still there and He knows whom you need around you. He also knows who needed to leave. Say good-bye to bad habits, negative people, unholy appetites, and impure thoughts. Say good-bye to laziness, lethargy, apathy, and doubt. I know that God is for me—and He is for you, too!

Journey Note

49 *Today's Gem*

If you are anything less than God intended you to be, you are not being true to the Lord. Your life is precious to Him and He doesn't want you to waste it on things that don't matter anymore. Things like what people say you'll never do or never become. Don't waste your life sulking over what you used to do or who you thought you would be by now. Sis, you are right where you are supposed to be, and on schedule. The Lord wants His vision to become your vision. He wants to make His heartbeat your heartbeat. He wants you to love what He loves and hate what He hates. Purpose to live as fully, as joyfully, and as meaningfully as possible. How? Through Jesus Christ. With Him, all things are possible and nothing is impossible.

Journey Note

50   *Today's Gem*

From a caterpillar to a butterfly—it's called process. This place you are in is God—it's not the devil. This experience is to certify that what God said about you is real and true. You are an awesome woman! You are clean! You are holy! You are pure—not because you earned it, but because of Him! Hold your head up and square your shoulders—you are royalty! Today is your day of restoration! It's been a long time coming, but change is here! Once you embrace this new place, you will realize it was well worth the wait. No more compromise! No more confusion! No more chaos! Change your posture; correct your position; condition your mind to receive the shift of God in your life! Today is your day of conversion—get ready to spread your wings and fly!

Journey Note

51  Today's Gem

Are you sick and tired of being sick and tired? When you really get to this point, you'll change! When you get truly disgusted with the guilt of waking up in the wrong bed, you'll change. When you get tired of picking up the pieces of your heart AGAIN, you'll change. When your head keeps chasing your heart through the same game—just a different name—and you discover "It's not them, it's me," you'll change. When Peter runs out of money to give you to pay Paul, and unnecessary debt is about to give you a nervous breakdown, you'll change. Bishop Noel Jones said, "Sometimes you have to almost lose your mind to change your mind." **Psalm 119:133** says, "Direct my steps by your word and let no iniquity have dominion over me." Get your life back!

Journey Note

52 *Today's Gem*

Does your image fit who God made you to be? At some point, every woman has a battle with herself. Whether it's comparing yourself to another woman's beauty, another woman's intelligence, or another woman's perceived happiness, these crossroads can often leave you wounded, dazed, and uncertain of your future. Often these encounters are God pulling at our deepest needs, and innermost thoughts and desires. God wants our most vulnerable places. He wants our past, our present, and our potential. Release who you think you should be and manifest who you are. Make room for God to ignite your future with the spark of His purpose, not your plans!

Journey Note

53 *Today's Gem*

God did not create you as an afterthought—you are an integral part of His plan in creation. Your uniqueness is a reflection of God's intent to impact the lives of those you come in contact with. You are God's idea. Do you really know how special you are, woman? Today, God wants to infiltrate your emptiness and fill you with Himself. God honors you. God respects you. God has great compassion for you. You are one of God's most precious jewels. You have great worth! You are royalty and you are seated right now in heavenly places—high above negative circumstances, negative people, and negative thoughts. **Philippians 2:5** states, "Let this mind be in you which was also in Christ Jesus." Why? Because God wants to release you from the box of your own thinking!

Journey Note

54 Today's Gem

Victims of domestic violence often feel shame and humiliation that this is happening to them. Victims of domestic violence often feel that they are the only ones who can change their mate and, consequently, feel protective of the relationship and responsible for keeping the family together. If you are a victim of domestic violence, you don't deserve abuse and *you are not alone*. You have the right to a relationship of mutual submission. **Ephesians 5:21** says, "Submit to one another out of reverence for Christ." Most importantly, you have the right to be free of fear. **Romans 8:15** states, "For you did not receive a spirit that makes you a slave again to fear, but you received the Spirit of Sonship. And by Him we cry, Abba Father." Sis, although you don't have control over your partner's violence, you do have a choice about how you respond to it.

Journey Note

55 *Today's Gem*

Far too many of us base our personal worth on what we believe the most important people in our lives think about us. We are constantly looking for someone else to tell us that we are significant. We look around to see who is watching us and spend far too much time wondering what they think. Well, God wants you to know that you are already whole and you are already complete in Him! Your value is NOT based on what somebody else thinks. It is based on what God says about you. **Ephesians 2:10** says, "We are His workmanship, created in Christ Jesus to do good works, which God prepared in advance for us to do." When your view of God changes, you will view yourself differently, too. Start here . . . God is an awesome God—if you are in Him and He is in you, guess what? You are awesome, too!

Journey Note

56 Today's Gem

In the words of pastor and author, Myles Monroe, "When a woman understands her purpose and how it relates to the man's purpose, she can bring much healing and fulfillment to her relationships. She may even be able to alleviate some of the situations of misuse and abuse in her own life." **Proverbs 19:21** says that "many plans are in a man's mind, but it is the Lord's purpose for him that will stand." Where purpose is unknown, abuse is inevitable. A woman who does not understand her purpose can be a detriment to a man, and a man who does not understand his purpose can be a detriment to a woman. Women, we were designed by God to be a powerful force for good in a man's life by being an encouragement to him. When women and men learn to live together harmoniously within their purpose and position, we will discover lasting contentment and fulfillment.

Journey Note

57 *Today's Gem*

Hey, Sis, don't just let life happen to you—participate. Either you prepare or you repair. Speaker and author, John Wooden said, "Too often, we exaggerate yesterday, we over-estimate tomorrow, which causes us to underestimate today. This mindset breeds procrastination. Reactive people repair and proactive people prepare." If you're not already, become a person with proper priorities and your future will be full of personal growth and unlimited potential. Make every day count—after all, it's the day the Lord has made.

Journey Note

58 *Today's Gem*

When you really get a revelation of who you are, your life will change. When you get an understanding of the power that is available to you, you'll no longer succumb to the "it just happened" moments orchestrated by the devil. When you will yourself to be whole, you make a commitment to the process of whatever it takes. In the words of Pastor Randy Morrison, "We are not human beings trying to have a spiritual experience. We are spiritual beings mastering the human existence."

Journey Note

59 Today's Gem

Soar, my sister, soar! God created you to be an eagle. Why are you walking around like a duck? You were created to fly above the storm, not beneath it. You were shaped and fashioned to look the enemy in the eyes and confront it head-on. No, don't avoid the pain of the process, but don't settle for it, either. You did not come this far for it to end like this. On the other side of "this" is redemption—God is going to bring you back. On the other side of "this" is restoration—God is going to give you more than you lost. On the other side of "this" is restitution—the joy you are about to have will make you forget the pain of this place. On the other side of "this" is true relationship with God, with yourself, and consequently with others.

Journey Note

60 *Today's Gem*

In order to move into your tomorrow, you must break your attachment to yesterday. When Christ becomes your EVERY-THING, He automatically displaces some people, places, and things. What is occupying space in your life that belongs to God? Who is pulling you away from what God said to you? Where are you going that you don't want your pastor to know about? *(As if God doesn't see you.)* Why are you chasing what doesn't belong to you when your steps are ordered by God? The Bible says in **Luke 12:32** "for it is your Father's good pleasure to give you the Kingdom." Come out of denial and bury those dead issues, relationships, situations, and memories. Allow God to activate the gift of release in your life—**LET IT GO!**

Journey Note

61   *Today's Gem*

In **John 14:21,** Jesus said that "The person who has my commands and keeps them is the one who really loves me; and whoever really loves Me will be loved by My Father; and I too will love him and will reveal Myself to Him. I will let Myself be clearly seen by him and make Myself real to him." Is Jesus real to you? Do you really love Him in your heart or is it just lip service? If you do, then why aren't you manifesting Him on earth with victory? Why do you continue to crucify Him over and over with your bad choices? Before you make another bad decision, ask yourself, *Will this choice please God?* If you get a release based on the Word of God, then you are on your way to another level of Sonship!

Journey Note

62   *Today's Gem*

If you go over your priorities you'll find what you've been missing. Have you been focusing on the things that really don't matter? **Proverbs 13:15–16** declares, "Good understanding gains favor, but the way of the unfaithful is hard. Every prudent man acts with knowledge, but a fool lays open his folly." Are you struggling with order in your life? If so, throw yourself on the altar of God and stay until He completes the word. **Proverbs 12:15** says, "The way of a fool is right in his own eyes, but he who heeds counsel is wise." Have you sought counsel lately?

Journey Note

63 Today's Gem

My daughter and I were watching *As Told by Ginger* on Nickelodeon television recently and the lyrics to the show open caught my attention. The song says, "Someone once told me the grass was much greener on the other side." After a moment I thought, *Yeah, the grass is much greener on the other side.* But guess what? The water bill is much higher, too! Paul said in **Philippians 4:11,** "Not that I am implying that I was in any personal want, for I have learned how to be content and satisfied to the point that I am not disturbed, regardless of my circumstances." Don't ever forget, girls, if God led you to it, He has plans to take you through it.

Journey Note

64   *Today's Gem*

    An anchor is a device that secures an object in place so that it becomes immobile. Like many women in the Body of Christ who have been on a turbulent journey, you've been tossed, turned, and tipped to the point that you have dropped an anchor in a place that God didn't intend for you to stay. You're stuck in discontentment and discouragement, and God is calling for you to come to contentment and encouragement. First you must release what God has already let go of! There is a terrible danger in holding on to what God has told you to let go of. Are you stuck in a place that does not make sense and that God did not ordain? You may be wounded, but you're still alive. Get up and get going—you might not enjoy the journey, but you are going to love the destination.

Journey Note

65   *Today's Gem*

Check your location! **Psalm 16:11** tells us that "In the presence of the Lord is fullness of joy." Our struggles, our challenges, and our quagmire is that often we are in the right place looking for the wrong thing or we are looking for the right thing in the wrong place. The end result is DRAMA! Drama is a series of happenings that seem so bizarre, or these occurrences are characterized by a dreamlike distortion of reality to the point that we live in illusions and consequently are robbed of the joy that rightfully belongs to us! We must all strive to keep the drama out of our lives.

Journey Note

66 *Today's Gem*

Mary J. Blige said in her hit song, "No More Drama" that she doesn't know where her story ends. But she knows where it begins! Where does your story begin? Better yet, where does your story begin again? It begins when we choose to walk in the authority and ability imputed to us through the finished work of Jesus Christ. It begins the moment you begin to make God choices, not just good choices. It begins the moment you agree with God's delays and detours in your life. **Jeremiah 29:11** encourages us with "For I know the thoughts and plans that I have for you, says the Lord, thoughts and plans for evil, to give you hope in your final outcome." I heard an awesome woman of God interpret **Romans 8:28** this way: If it's not all good, then God ain't finished!

Journey Note

67 *Today's Gem*

From today forward, all things have purpose. Every area of our lives should push us toward purpose. God wants us to be women of purpose, driven by purpose. He does not want us to be driven by passion only, for passion is just the fuel that drives purpose. He does not want us to be driven by hidden agendas or unpure motives, for these seeds ultimately produce a painful harvest. We cannot write the script for our lives. When you really walk in purpose—God's purpose—you put your agenda on the shelf and declare HOWEVER, WHATEVER, WHENEVER, Lord. I'm totally devoted to You.

Journey Note

68 *Today's Gem*

It's time to move on, girl. When God has a mission for you, He'll do whatever it takes to get you there. Before He'll let you miss out on your destiny, He'll permit trouble to uproot you. In fact, you may be going through certain difficulties right now because you are trying to stay where you are, not where you're supposed to be. You can't freeze-frame your past or re-live it. What's done is done. What's gone is gone. What's over is over—let it go and move on. When God moves, you must learn to move with Him. Take what's left and move forward. What's waiting for you is BIGGER and BETTER than what you can imagine.

Journey Note

69 *Today's Gem*

Sis, you can't relive your past. If you could, you would be able to undo the pain—and just maybe, things would be different. The irony is that we need pain, problems, and mistakes to become who we are. The beauty is that God has made provisions for the annoyances of life. Mistakes are a part of the training. God is a personal God and He is committed to your finish. Instead of wiping you out and using someone else, He made provision for your restoration. Stop wading around in what could have been and take advantage of the opportunity to do it better the next time.

Journey Note

70 *Today's Gem*

God's ultimate purpose for us is found in **Genesis 1:28** where we are commanded to "be fruitful, multiply, replenish, subdue, and have dominion." The more we embrace God's purpose, the less we feel the pain of being processed for purpose. Embracing purpose causes us to "grow" through, what we "go" through, instead of complaining and becoming bitter. **Romans 12:2** tells us to "be not conformed to this world, but be ye transformed by the renewing of your mind." Wrap your mind around that bit of information and let the Holy Spirit breathe on it so that you can receive it with joy! Once you embrace it, this truth, make the change. Transformation is the ultimate goal of revelation.

Journey Note

71 *Today's Gem*

The key to beauty for Kingdom women is found in **1 Peter 3:4,** which states, "Instead, it should be that of your inner self, the unfading beauty of a gentle and quiet spirit, which is of great worth in God's sight." This kind of beauty gets better the older it gets. God describes beautiful as wisdom, kindness, gentleness, virtue, and godliness. **Proverbs 31:30** says that "charm is deceptive and external beauty is fleeting (it comes and goes); but a woman who fears the Lord is to be praised." Very few women fear the Lord. To marry a prince, you must first become a princess! As you set your attention on developing godly character and a pure heart, Christ will transform you into the beautiful princess He created you to be. God wants to make you ready for what He already has ready for YOU!

Journey Note

72 $\quad$ *Today's Gem*

The best way to get through is to go through. Not over, not under, not around—but all the way through it. The phrase "And it came to pass" is found in the Word of God 430 times. It did not come to stay—it came to keep going. But you invited it to stay. **Ecclesiastes 3:1** tells us, "To everything there is a season, and a time for every matter or purpose under heaven." Don't stop now; you're almost there. You are closer to coming out than you are if you turn back to where you came from. Push your way, press your way, praise your way—for when you come out on the other side of this, your promise is waiting for you.

Journey Note

73 *Today's Gem*

It's time to rise up! God often allows the enemy to come against us with such great intensity so that we can be provoked to use what's in us. You are not just a great woman. But you are also a graceful warrior! You're anointed to resist the devil. You are anointed to rule and reign. You are commanded not just to be fruitful, multiply, and subdue — but you are also commanded to have dominion. You don't have to take what you already have. Can you let go of "whatever" to say yes to God? Can you let go of "whomever" to show God how much you love Him? It's after salvation. Now what? Come out of your comfort zone — Zion is calling you to a higher place.

Journey Note

74 *Today's Gem*

Are you a woman who has discovered that you are the apple of God's eye, therefore, you can ask what you will and it shall be given unto you? Or are you a woman who has settled into a posture of complacency and thus you settle for and accept WHATEVER comes your way? **Proverbs 10:22** declares, "The blessing of the Lord, it maketh rich, and he addeth no sorrow with it." If you are experiencing more sorrow than joy, maybe you ought to investigate the source of the gift. God wants to move you into another dimension of His goodness. Engage, embrace, and endure this transition you are in. Decide to expose yourself to nothing less than God's best! God wants to bridge some gaps in your life. Today, God wants to give you a mind to recover your self-worth. He wants you to reclaim your rightful place in Him and rejoice, for every scar on your reputation has become an instrument in the symphony of His glory in your life.

Journey Note

75 *Today's Gem*

Make that decision today that you have been putting off. You are worried about things that you have no control over. Make the decision and let God work out the details. The pain of the choice you have to make is temporary. God will give you grace to endure the discomfort and courage to hold your ground. You have the power to "undo" some things! What do you do when your heart's desire is not God's will? Agree with God. **Proverbs 13:15** says that the way of the transgressor is hard! I'll tell you this: when the pain of the challenge becomes greater than the pain of the choice you have to make, you'll change. The good news is this: weeping may endure for a night, but joy comes in the morning. Your decision releases your morning!

Journey Note

76 *Today's Gem*

There is a blessing for you today in the unexpected! But first, you must thank God for where you are. Then, and only then, will God release you into the next place of His glory. Things are not as bad as they seem. What you have focused on is the delusive appearance and attempt of the enemy of your soul to shake your faith. Like the woman with the issue of blood, when you get desperate enough to touch God, your faith will make you whole. To get through what you are going through, look at what you cannot see with the natural eye. See yourself in the next place of blessing—holy, healed, and happy!

Journey Note

77  Today's Gem

Stop! It's time for a change. You have been doing the same thing, the same way, for too long, getting the same results. But today God wants to break your routine and cast you into the unusual. Cancel the devil's success in your life. Go a different way. Break your attachment to yesterday—it's holding up your future. Is it a person that never has anything positive to say? Is it a habit that's killing you? Is it a friendship that has outlived its season in your life? Is it memories from the past that keep you from, instead of pushing you to? Stop rehearsing the past! The word of God tells us to "Lay aside every weight and the sin that so easily besets us." Girl, get yourself together and move on! I challenge you to risk having nothing for a moment. In exchange, God will gather you and all your broken pieces, and will blow your mind with blessings. You can't imagine the great things that are coming your way!

Journey Note

78 Today's Gem

If Christ is the center of your life like you say He is, then why are you anxious? Why are you fearful? Worry is a warning light on the dashboard of your spirit that Christ has been shoved to the sideline. . . .

Journey Note

79 _Today's Gem_

The season of defeat would be over in your life if you would just activate the Word of God. The season of struggle would be over in your life if you would just actualize the promises of God. If God said it, that settles it. God knows that. The devil knows that. But do you know that, Sis? God's will is stronger than any force on Earth, and His will is available to work in your life if you would just agree with God. The moment you agree with God's will for your life is the moment your life changes. Why? Because in this dimension of restoration, you can expect unexpected blessings.

Journey Note

80 Today's Gem

Philippians 3:13–14 declares, "I do not consider sisters, that I have captured and made it my own yet; but one thing I do: forgetting what lies behind and straining forward to what lies ahead, I press . . ." This is a season of good-byes and hellos. Good-bye to the old and hello to the new. Good-bye to unholy appetites and hello to righteousness. Good-bye to illicit relationships and hello to Godly covenants. Good-bye to famine and hello to more than enough. Good-bye to depression and hello to joy everlasting. Good-bye to mental anguish and hello to peace that surpasses all understanding. Today is your day to walk into your season . . . of hello!

Journey Note

81 *Today's Gem*

Good morning, girls. Somebody listening needs to know that today you can begin again. Today is your chance to get it right; to make it right. **Lamentations 3** provides hope for your hopeless situation. Increase your capacity to receive more of God by faith. It is because of the Lord's mercies that we are not consumed, because His compassions are not like man's—they fail not. They are new every morning—sufficient for today! Therefore, hope in Him! Right now, receive strength to trust Him; strength to submit to Him; strength to surrender all of your baggage, burdens, and bondages. Today, purpose not to be a slave to your soulish desires, emotions, and unholy appetites! **Psalm 107:8–9** says, "Oh, that men would praise the Lord for His goodness and for His wonderful works to the children of men. For He alone satisfies the longing soul and fills the hungry soul with good."

Journey Note

82 *Today's Gem*

Lord, help us as women to be at peace with Your pace in our lives. Help us to realize that sometimes we must forfeit what we think is good to get what You know is best. Help us to accept that often our agenda does not match Yours, and therefore we must endure temporary heartache and pain due to the loss of what we thought was necessary to survive. Give us spiritual insight to rest in the fact that every now and then we must disconnect to reconnect. Ladies, we are in a season of rearranging, readjusting, and reevaluating. Know this and persuade your soul to agree. **Psalm 138:8** states, "The Lord will perfect that which concerns me!" If God started it, He will finish it—and all that God does is ON TIME!

Journey Note

83 *Today's Gem*

Are you trying to fit into a space not designed to accommodate you? It feels like you're trying to force a square into a triangle. Girl, that's why it's so painful. Few things hurt more than a gorgeous pair of shoes that are too small. It causes your whole body to ache. Likewise, our entire lives are affected when we try to fit our dreams, hopes, desires, and plans into a space that cannot accommodate the vastness of God's intent for our lives. The nudging, the urging, the rumbling, the lack of peace is God conveying to you that you are not in the space He created for you, so don't get comfortable. The peace you seek will come—when you agree with your purpose on purpose.

Journey Note

84 *Today's Gem*

Don't disrespect your vulnerability! Acknowledge it so you can deal with it realistically. Don't be afraid of it—confront it so you can overcome it. Don't ignore it, for then you become a candidate for abuse. You are more than a survivor—you're an overcomer. So, ladies, live in your purpose on purpose! God has need of you and your testimony. He wants you to be excellent! He wants you to be an example. Remember, in Him you live, move, and have your being. Oh, yeah, and in Him your vulnerability becomes an asset—how? In our weakness, He's made strong!

Journey Note

85   *Today's Gem*

If you are living in black and white, God wants to color your world with praise. Praise summons God to your *blah*ness. Yes, I made that up! The key here is that God's presence is full of joy. Therefore, I surrender the stress of my situation to a posture of total praise. Why? Because praise confuses the devil! To determine the value of an item, one gets an appraisal (which comes from the root word *praise*). Thus, praise determines the value of God's power, God's place, and God's presence in your life. Praise Him until your situation manifests a rainbow. What? Yes, color your world with praise and watch the promises of God begin to come to pass in your life.

Journey Note

86 *Today's Gem*

I don't know who you are, but listen up—you've come too far to miss God now. The call of God in your life is greater than the fall in your life. Mistakes don't delete destiny—giving up does. Refuse to look like your situation! Don't lose what God has for you because of people's opinions. You choose whose opinions impact your life. Choose to believe what God has said about you. That may challenge you to even stretch beyond what you believe about yourself. It's not your failure that makes you achieve or not achieve. It's your response to the failure. Benjamin Franklin said it this way: "The things which hurt are the best instructors in the world." Now learn the lesson and get moving.

Journey Note

87  Today's Gem

You were called to do the ridiculous. That means you've been called to do what has never been done before. Don't worry about being equipped—for God promised to supply all our needs according to His riches in glory. When God calls ordinary people to do extraordinary work, you will be ridiculed. Remember Noah? God called Noah to build a boat in a place that had never experienced water. The people thought Noah was crazy for obeying God. In the end, Noah's obedience saved his life and it changed his life. Sis, what is God calling you to that has never been done before?

Journey Note

88 *Today's Gem*

God wants to expand your vision of who you are. You are a woman of might and power, uniquely designed by God to birth His will and purpose on Earth. You are a good woman! So take courage and embrace your strength. Get excited and stay excited about life. Enjoy giving and receiving love—you deserve it. Face and transform your fears and turn them into faith. Ask for help when you need it—it's a sign of strength, not weakness. Spring free of the superwoman trap. Trust God to help you make your own choices and decisions. Become your own best friend. Complete unfinished business. Realize that you have emotional and practical rights. Talk as nicely to yourself as you do to your plants. Want more? Tune in tomorrow, but today, love yourself fully. For you are an awesome woman!

Journey Note

89 *Today's Gem*

Who is "they"? Where do "they" live? Why do "they" matter? If God said it, what does their opinion have to do with it? Haven't you allowed "they" to hinder your forward movement long enough? You don't have to fear "they"; what "they" can do, or what "they" say! Some 99.9 percent of the time, "they" aren't going to help you anyway! "They" are just in the way of what God wants to do in your life. "They" work for the devil and mean you only evil. So today, STOP listening to "they" and START listening to what God has said about you. STOP explaining your obedience to God and START looking for God to open new doors and shut old ones! **Psalm 41:11** says, "By this I know that the Lord favors me and delights in me, because my enemies do not triumph over me!"

Journey Note

90 *Today's Gem*

What would you do if you were not afraid? Would you start a business? Would you leave an abusive relationship? Would you end a needy friendship? Would you go back to school? Would you pursue purchasing a home? Would you meet new people? Would you get help for that addiction? The Bible says in **2 Timothy 1:7** that God has not given us "the spirit of fear, but of power, love and sound mind." The sum of all fears is destiny delayed! Today, God wants YOU to "flip the script." Instead of adding all your fears, think about what He has already done for you, and be encouraged by the sum of all your faith!

Journey Note

91 *Today's Gem*

I was reading an article by Max Lucado and he asked a question that I found quite interesting. The question was, "Do you have worry-itis?" Worry divides the mind. Anxiety splits your energy between today's priorities and tomorrow's problems. He said, "Part of your mind is on the now; the rest in on the not-yet and the result is half-minded living. Although worrying isn't a disease, it causes diseases such as high blood pressure, heart trouble, migraine headaches, and a host of stomach disorders, to name a few. Worry doesn't work—so stop using it. The Bible says in **1 Peter 5:7**, "Cast your care upon Him for He cares for you." Let God handle whatever you are concerned about. God said He would! Either you believe Him or you don't.

Journey Note

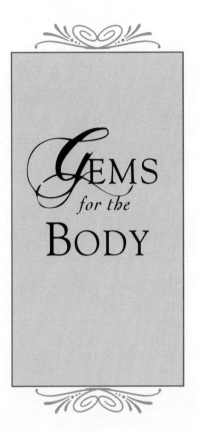

GEMS
for the
BODY

92 *Today's Gem*

Most of us are familiar with **Psalm 139:14,** which tells us that we are fearfully and wonderfully made. But do you really know what that means? It means that when God created you, He created a masterpiece. There is no one else like you. Your eyes, your hair, your voice, your smile, your size, your style, your personality—it's uniquely you. You are peculiar! You are exclusively His and He has great plans for you! You are the praise of His glory! You are an example of God's intent to change the world! Yes, you! So today, put your ear to God's mouth. Listen carefully . . . He wants to tell you something about you that amazes you! If God drops it in your mind, then rest assured it's in your future. God made you who you are to do what He has called you to do. Are you looking for your identity? Guess what? It's in Christ!

Journey Note

93 *Today's Gem*

   Women's health is a complex paradigm. I read recently in a newspaper article that our health is influenced by biology, psychology, sociology, sexuality, and spirituality. The number one health issue facing women today is being everything to everyone else and neglecting ourselves shamelessly for the approval of others. Eating disorders, cancer, anxiety, phobias, depression, stress, and other physiological diseases are nothing but separation from self. It's called perfectionism! Sis, the only one who can effectively be all things to all people is God. Ask God to point you in the direction of your purpose and live. God gives grace for purpose. If you're always tired and running out of time, you are doing too much. God is not going to fix that—He's leaving that to you.

Journey Note

94 *Today's Gem*

Life teaches us many things, ladies, if we would just avail ourselves of its tutoring. **Proverbs 19:8** says, "She who gains wisdom loves her own life; she who keeps understanding shall prosper and find good." Wisdom means knowing how to apply truth in every situation. I came across a piece of wisdom shared by author Veronica Shoffstall, which said, "Even sunshine burns if you get too much." So instead of waiting for someone to bring you flowers, plant your own garden and decorate your own life. After every good-bye, every mistake, every missed opportunity, COMMIT TO NEVER STOP LEARNING.

Journey Note

95 *Today's Gem*

Dreams are what get you started; discipline is what keeps you going. Girl, don't quit. "Success is failure turned inside out, the silver tint of the clouds of doubt. You can never tell how close you are—it may be near when it seems so far. So stick to the fight when you are hardest hit—it's when things are the toughest that you must not quit." In the familiar poem this unknown author was conveying that failure is simply an opportunity to start over and try harder! So start that business, go back to school, finish that project, submit that idea, reach for the stars. Honey, your job is to take care of the possible and to trust God with the impossible.

Journey Note

96 *Today's Gem*

As women, most of us are very busy. Our natural tendencies are to hit the floor running each morning, ready to tackle the day. However, in order to successfully have a productive day, we must realize that life management is really spiritual management. **John 15:5** tells us that without Him, we can do nothing. So, Sis, each day, take care of first things first. Aim at giving the first minutes of each day to God by reading His word. David said in **Psalm 63:1,** "Early will I seek You, my soul thirsts for You." This discipline will ensure sustenance, nutrition, and energy for the day.

Journey Note

97   *Today's Gem*

    You are the prize. You are the queen. You are the daughter of a King, so that makes you a princess. You deserve the absolute best that God has tailor-made for you. You are precious. You are the treasure. True contentment is learned. You are a vessel of honor . . . a pearl of great price. Look in the mirror — you are a reflection of God's grace and ingenuity. When He created you, God put that mold away. There is no one else like you — anywhere. Expect to be treated like royalty and act like the princess you are.

Journey Note

98 *Today's Gem*

Holiness does not mean long dresses, no makeup, no jewelry, or no fun. Holiness means wholeness, healthy, fulfilled, full of unspeakable joy, and available to God. Holiness means you love what God loves and hate what He hates. Holiness means you are pliable or flexible to His will. Holiness means trusting God to give you what and who you need, even if that manifestation doesn't reflect what you think you want! **Jeremiah 29:11** assures us that God has plans for us that are going to bless us beyond what we can even imagine! However, in order to receive it, you must surrender everything. Come on, Sis, risk having nothing for a moment, so that you can have it all.

Journey Note

99   *Today's Gem*

A good friend recently told me that men often live and regret that they made no time for their children as they were growing up. However, women quite often live and regret that they made no time for themselves. That doesn't have to happen to you, Sis. From today forward, take time for yourself—every day. Whether it's an early-morning stroll or a late-evening cup of tea—take time for yourself. It could be a monthly massage or a biweekly manicure—take time for you. Perhaps it's thirty minutes alone with a great book, or an unexpected phone call to a friend. Girl, you are everything to everyone else. Now it's time to treat yourself like the image of Christ you are—with tender, loving care.

Journey Note

100 Today's Gem

Are you dressed for success? No, I'm not talking about your Jones New York suit and your designer shoes. I'm not referring to your perfect accessories, MAC makeup, and fresh perm. When you looked in the mirror this morning, were you clothed in humility and love? Were you properly accessorized with joy, peace, long-suffering, kindness, goodness, and self-control? Did you cover up with the garment of praise? Good, because God wants you to model for Him today! Go, girl— walk with the confidence of God. **1 Peter 3:4** says that "incorruptible beauty comes from a gentle and quiet spirit." This is what makes you precious to God, Sis!

Journey Note

101 *Today's Gem*

Are you a woman who keeps herself busy—too busy for your own good? What's "too busy for your own good"? It's when you make time for working eight hours a day, leave work, go straight to church, leave church, get home just in time to grab a late-night snack, sleep for a few hours—only to start the race again! "Too busy" is when you mistake church work for the work of ministry, but your husband and children feel neglected. "Too busy" is when you substitute religious activity for relationship with God, and therefore you have voids in your heart that you fill with the wrong thing or the wrong person. "Too busy" is when you work harder than you ever have and still you don't accomplish much. Well, today, God wants to rearrange your life—stand still and embrace God's agenda for your life.

Journey Note

102 Today's Gem

It's time to get your house in order. There are some things that God wants to release to you, but He won't because you're not prepared to receive. He wants to bless you financially—but you are irresponsible with what you have. Do you balance your checkbook, do you pay your tithes, do you pay your bills on time, are you in unnecessary debt? You say you want a house—but you don't even clean your apartment. Or maybe you want to own your own business—but you struggle to get to your current job on time. Well, Sis, when preparation meets opportunity, promotion takes place. Develop a plan; exercise patience, and endure the process. For only after you're found faithful over a few things, will He make you ruler over much.

Journey Note

103 *Today's Gem*

How often do you REALLY clean your house? I mean wash the windows, polish the wood, clean the mirrors, sweep the floors, and change the linen? Okay—how often do you clean your house? I mean get an annual checkup; monitor your hygiene; take care of your hair, skin, and nails; exercise, eat right; release stress; and pamper yourself? Seriously, how often do you clean your house? I mean read the Word, talk to God, listen to God, reevaluate relationships, and repent? Sure, it takes a lot more time to really clean your house than it does to quickly cover up and straighten up! Today, purpose to take time, make time, find the time to let God clean what you've been covering.

Journey Note

104 Today's Gem

What do little girls see when they look at you? Do they see a strong, intelligent woman who is honest with herself and others? Or do they see a little girl in a woman's body who is bitter, silly, and always blaming other people for her decisions and indecisions? What do little girls see when they observe our interaction with each other? Do they see friendship, support, encouragement, and loyalty? Or do they see treachery, betrayal, jealousy, and disrespect? Woman of God—in Christ, through Christ, you have the chance to impact a generation when we walk in purpose—on purpose. Remember, some little girl is watching you!

Journey Note

105 *Today's Gem*

Are you tired of being tired all the time? With all that you do it still seems like you haven't done enough. The husband, the kids, the job, the house, the ministry—oh, yeah (every now and then a minute for yourself!). Well, take a moment and reevaluate what is important to you. Often, we discover that what we want is quite frequently not what is best for us. With God, you work less, yet you accomplish more. As a garden needs to be cultivated, so does your life. A neglected plant withers—a neglected life withers, too! Purpose to take time each day for yourself. A little prayer, praise, and pampering go a long, long way!

Journey Note

106 Today's Gem

As women we are nurturers by nature. The ability of a woman to be tenderhearted was in God's creative design. God designed women to be communicators. We love to talk, and we love to listen. Well, today I want to encourage you to listen to your body! We take care of everybody else, but today, I want to redirect your focus back to your temple. You have a very special guest residing in your temple. How can you house the most precious gift known to mankind if you continue to neglect yourself? You can't! How can you be effective in the Kingdom of God if you are always tired? You can't! How can you walk into the fullness of your womanhood if you don't do the practical things like drink water, exercise, visit your gynecologist annually, and get proper rest? Ladies, listen to your body. When you walk intimately with the Lord, you are never caught off guard. What has your body been telling you lately?

Journey Note

107 *Today's Gem*

Relax and just be! Be the jewel God made you—look pretty and wait on God to set you in place. You don't have to convince anyone that they need you around. If it takes too much energy, too much persuading, too much maneuvering, too much adjusting, that's not it. That's not the mate; that's not the friend; that's not the mentor; that's not the covenant connection God had in mind. Stop going around the divine roadblocks He has in place—there's a reason for them. You can only see what's in front of you, but God can see around the corner. Relax, and release your future to the Father. Don't worry—He's perfecting all that concerns you.

Journey Note

108 *Today's Gem*

You are God's idea! Anything God thought of and created is already valuable. You belong to God. Therefore, when you need affirmation, approval, or admiration, reflect on what you came from (royalty); remember who you came from (the King of Kings); recall why you came (to fulfill purpose and destiny assigned by God Himself). Therefore, your identity and worth are NOT based on where you live, whom you marry, or what you do. Because you live, move, and have your being in Christ. Stop striving—**JUST BE!**

Journey Note

109 *Today's Gem*

I want to talk about domestic violence. Yes, domestic violence comes to church, too. It is the systematic pattern of physical, sexual, emotional, or psychological abusive behaviors used in a relationship by one partner to control another. In addition to violent physical contact, some other examples of abuse are neglect, repetitious degradation—always putting you down—false accusations, playing mind games, destroying trust, limiting reproductive freedom, and extreme jealousy, to name a few. But God wants you to know that you are not responsible for causing this behavior and it is **NOT** His will for your life. **1 Peter 3:7** states, "Husbands, in the same way be considerate as you live with your wives, and treat them with respect." You have the **right** to receive respect from your mate.

Journey Note

110 Today's Gem

I remember growing up and bopping my head to Chaka Khan's hit song "You Should Be Thankful for What You've Got." Now that song has new meaning to me. Too often we look with envy at other people's success, other people's prosperity, other people's families, other people's marriages and ministries, etc. But the reality is that you don't know the cost of that alabaster box. You don't know the pain, the pressure, or the process that was endured to get to that point. Look back over your life—what have YOU survived? Look at your life now—what do you have that would be a blessing to someone else? And finally, look into your future—the moment you find contentment where you are is the moment your future expands.

Journey Note

111 Today's Gem

    I want to challenge you today to pursue excellence—not just success. You can be successful with a less-than-excellent representation of the Kingdom. Excellence is knowing that you chose God over choosing him or her to attain your status. Success built on deception ultimately crumbles. Unfortunately, some sisters use their "successful bodies" to drive a Lexus, shop at Nordstroms, travel around the country, and enjoy the "good life." Excellence is manifesting a deeper level of Christ in your daily walk. Excellence is having clean hands and a pure heart. When you pursue excellence, success will come. And the best part of it is, the only thing you have to give up, girl, is your best praise!

Journey Note

112 *Today's Gem*

Destiny is not a haphazard plan of God! It's often a painful process. But in the midst of that pain we often discover our function in ministry. God's purpose is not hindered by your past. The passageway to destiny is a tight place. Your commitment to your calling is what gives you the power to overcome your struggle. You are anointed to outlive your mistakes. Your experiences make your testimony effective. Aretha Franklin said it this way: "A rose is still a rose, and baby girl, you are still a flower!" Thorns don't make the rose ugly. Thorns make you handle the rose with much more care. You are a woman of destiny, and today is your turning point!

Journey Note

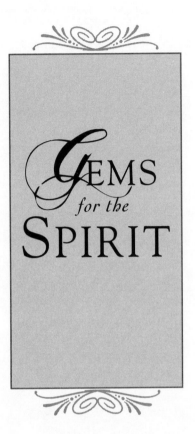

Gems
for the
Spirit

113 *Today's Gem*

Take inventory of your relationships and your environment. Who is in your life that the Lord didn't assign to your life? What is in your life that God didn't put there? These questions are not about friendship and comfort, but about purpose. Every relationship in your life should work for the cause of Christ. **Proverbs 13:20** says, "She who walks with the wise grows wise, but a companion of fools suffers harm." Often the choice for a deeper commitment to Christ produces resentment from people who used to be "close friends." You mirror those who influence you. Are you willing to be like Ruth and move away from all that is familiar? Are you willing to take a journey with Jesus toward the complete unknown? Think about it this way. "Relocation" positions you for "revelation," which ultimately manifests "restoration."

Journey Note

114 Today's Gem

I was talking to my godmother and she made a profound statement. She said, "Vikki, a lonely woman is like a drowning man—she'll reach for anything!" Sis, what have you reached for lately that's not a part of God's plan for you? What have you taken ownership of that doesn't belong to you? If you take a prescription that belongs to someone else, it has the potential to be fatal. Stop grabbing at everything that comes by and stop hearing what's not being said. When it's yours, girlie girl, it will identify itself clearly—in other words, if you have to ask, that's not it.

Journey Note

115 *Today's Gem*

Are we too busy with church work that we miss opportunity for ministry? How many times, on our way to church, have we passed people who needed ministry? How many hungry people have we ignored on our way to eat? As we seek to work out our purpose and destiny, let's not forget to include the gift of compassion. Compassion will provoke you to stop and do something that seems insignificant to you but will be life changing for someone else. I was sitting in a seminar once and the speaker concluded his session with the quote: You may be only one person to the world; but God has prepared at least one person for your life to impact, and it will mean the world." Do something for somebody today who can't repay you!!!

Journey Note

116 Today's Gem

Lately, God has impressed upon me to bridge the gap and create opportunities for intergenerational exchange. **Titus 2:3–5** admonishes older women to train younger women. Whether you call them church mothers, mothers in Zion, women of wisdom, or seasoned sisters, they are hidden treasures full of value. They can pass down knowledge, experience, training, and encouragement. Whatever you need, God has someone who can and wants to meet that need. Maybe you are full of oil to share with a young woman in Christ. Whether you're giving or receiving, this is the season to pass the torch and bridge the gap.

Journey Note

117  *Today's Gem*

Real friends are those who, when you've made a fool of yourself, don't feel you've done a permanent job. Today, I want to celebrate the sista circles, the sista girl network, the sista summits, the sista friends who always care enough to give their best. The girlfriends who never wait for an invitation, or they just show up when we need them most. A woman's ability to nurture friendships is her lifeline. A real friend brings out the best in you. Often, friends do what family can't or won't do. Friends are not judgmental and are like a second self. Friends are often the way God sends help, comfort, relief, and joy. Always make time for your sista friends—it's like making time for yourself.

Journey Note

118 *Today's Gem*

You are like the pearl of great price. Expensive! Valuable! Worthy! Unique! Peculiar! Precious! Therefore, when a man truly loves you, he will be willing to pay the price to secure you in his life forever. **Matthew 13:46** tells of the dealer who, on finding a single pearl of great price, went and sold all he had and bought it. Mama used to say a man won't buy the cow if he can get the milk for free. Premature sexual encounters rob women of so much—security, true joy, and virtue. You are the Lord's choice. Now sit back, relax, and wait on God's choice for you!

Journey Note

119 *Today's Gem*

The love of God is not like the love of the last man that hurt you. Change your mind about God. Change your view of God. He is the frame of reference. He is the original lover of your soul. In Him you are perfect, pure, and precious. Can't nobody love you like He can. He knows all of your stuff—your insecurities, your vulnerabilities—and He still loves you. He won't lie to you. He won't leave you. He keeps His promises—even when you don't expect Him to do so. Stop looking for a man to complete you as a woman. Seek ye first the Kingdom of God and all His righteousness. After you do that you'll receive everything else—including a love the way God intended.

Journey Note

120 Today's Gem

In a recent conversation with a male family member and a subsequent discussion with a male friend, I was told the reason they were not married or in a potential life partnership is because women don't like nice guys. They both said women only respond to "thug lovin'" or bad boys. To hear that from two different men at two different times made me curious. Why is it that women get bored with "nice guys"? I submit to you today that it's because abnormal has become normal and dysfunction has become our comfort zone. Honey, it was never God's intention for you to get caught up with a boy in a man's body. Don't get hoodwinked by the devil. . . . When the grass looks greener next door . . . water your own!

Journey Note

121 Today's Gem

God wants to put the family back in order. It's time for us as women to get rid of the "Amazon mentality." Amazons were a legendary culture of warrior women who dominated men. The devil has perpetuated that mind-set and produced a generation of bossy women who are robbing their men and themselves of the perfect relationships God has planned for both men and women. Women, stop mothering your men (let go and let God). Men, step up and take your rightful place as leaders, protectors, and providers. God created us for each other in our respective roles. Real women want real men—it's the plan and design of God.

Journey Note

122  *Today's Gem*

When a man really loves you, Sis, you'll know it. You won't have to guess. If he leaves, he'll come back. If he stays, it's because he wants to do so. Girl, just be the prize you are. Wait silently and patiently on God. Not a man, not a ring, not a wedding . . . Wait on God. Giving your heart to God avoids heartbreak, heartache, and devastation. However, be honest with God—pour out your unfulfilled desires at His feet. Why? Jesus will turn your pain and unbridled passion into purpose, power, and the promise of a fulfilled future.

Journey Note

123 Today's Gem

Several years ago, Yolanda Adams released a song entitled "What About the Children?" Today, the Lord is challenging us to get ourselves together for the children. The privilege to touch a child's life—whatever your role—is the privilege to touch a nation. Children oftentimes carry the guilt and blame for serious problems that affect their families. Why? Because through their fantasy of power, they believe that they are both the cause and effect, that they have the power to change their situation for better or for worse. So if you're struggling to make some changes in your life for the better, if you can't do it for yourself, do it for the children.

Journey Note

124 Today's Gem

Are you a woman who loves too much? How do you know? Often you are an expert in promoting the well-being of others but you are unfamiliar with ways of securing your own. Drama and chaos are always present, and therefore are necessary for you to be comfortable. Peace and quiet are awkward. You pay more attention to someone else's welfare than your own! You jump from relationship to relationship because being alone is more painful than the worst pain of any relationship. STOP! Right now God is offering you the chance to trade the temporary excitement of turmoil for the permanent satisfaction of intimacy with Him.

Journey Note

125 *Today's Gem*

This is not the season to be dislocated. Dislocation produces a lack of circulation that ultimately manifests an infection that can cause death if not treated immediately. Dislocation is painful. However, when you are connected properly, **Ephesians 4:16** declares that "you grow to full maturity and are able to be built up in love." Get connected to the right person, to the right church, to the right vision so God can bring forth purpose in you. You've been wandering long enough. Purpose is calling you back to where you belong—to fulfill the purpose for which you were born.

Journey Note

126  Today's Gem

Somebody in your sphere of influence is waiting on God. Guess what? God is waiting on you. You are the answer to somebody's questions. You are the solution to somebody's problem. God has blessed you to be a blessing. God has love flowing through you so that you can show the love of God to somebody else. God has given you joy, gentleness, and peace so that you can speak the peace of God and joy everlasting to a sister or brother in Christ. God has need of you, Woman of God. Yes, you. You don't need a pulpit. You don't need a license. You don't even need a microphone. Simply share your story, Sis—you went through that to help somebody else. You want to know your purpose? Look back over your life and recall your points of pain. That was boot camp—this is the REAL thing!

Journey Note

127 *Today's Gem*

Have you ever been in love with someone who was in love with someone else? Have you ever tried to capture someone's attention whose focus was in another direction? If your answer is yes, then you know firsthand how God feels every time He whispers your name to draw close to Him and you ignore Him or you are too busy. God is calling us to examine our hearts. Yes, you are saved, but are you fully committed? Yes, you go to church every Sunday and may even be in leadership, but is God sharing your heart with something or someone that has become an idol? Reconnect to your first love and you'll reconnect to your passion, your power, and your purpose.

Journey Note

128 *Today's Gem*

Proverbs 17:17 proclaims that "a friend loves at all times and a sister is born for times of adversity." When everything is going well, don't ever worry about being alone—there will always be a crowd. However, real, true friends are endearing and enduring—they are loyal. Good friends are for bad times. True friends rejoice when you succeed and remind you of God's goodness and faithfulness when you fail. So take a moment and evaluate whom you call friend. In this season of multiple transitions, you need to know who is around you and why. Need a jump start? Think back to lean times and remember who was there for you to lean on.

Journey Note

129  *Today's Gem*

Is your relationship with God being hindered because of your relationship with people? **Matthew 6:14–15** says that "your heavenly Father will forgive you as you forgive others. But if you don't forgive others, neither will your Father forgive you." Is your purpose and destiny being held up because you choose not to release an offense? Is that person really worth you not receiving what God has for you? God knows it hurts. He knows you feel that your anger, resentment, and bitterness are justified. But listen, Sis, it's blocking the pathway to your promise. Take a spiritual laxative today and flush out the soul—which is the realm of your emotions. I assure you, what's coming is better than what's been.

Journey Note

130 *Today's Gem*

It's in a woman's nature to be a nurturer. God created us with breasts that give life. Be careful what you draw to your life-giving source! You must stop nursing dead memories, dead issues, dead relationships, dead attachments, sickly habits, and ungodly desires. **Philippians 3:13–14** states, "forgetting what lies behind and straining forward to what lies ahead, I press on toward the goal." You have purpose. Stop waiting on what's not coming. It's time to dismiss yesterday so your tomorrow can live. Let that thing go. God's got something else for you. And what you see in your mind—it's greater than that!

Journey Note

131 *Today's Gem*

God didn't bring you this far to get leftovers. You are too precious to be some man's pit stop on the weekend or whenever he can spare some time away from his wife. You are better than that! God wants to bless you with wholeness—and then with someone who values all of you. Cheap relationships are demeaning and belittling. Cheap relationships chip away at your self-worth. God already knows the hardest things to release are the things you didn't expect to lose. Bring your broken heart, broken hopes, and broken dreams—bring all your broken pieces to a whole God. He wants to restore what you've lost and remind you of what's waiting for you—in Him!

Journey Note

132 Today's Gem

Ladies, we were created for intimacy. In the midst of intimacy, women come alive. Whether it is with good friends, our spouse, our children, or Jesus, intimacy reveals the tenderness locked inside. Intimacy with Christ positions us to pour out and to be poured into without being needy. Intimacy produces unspeakable joy, undisturbed composure, and unbelievable peace. Intimacy is proof of connection in thought, heart, and spirit. We know the blessings of the Lord. We are familiar with His exploits and recognize His Word. But do you know Him? Often, we as women invite men into our hearts before they invite us into their lives. Well, today, experience the ultimate intimacy — God is inviting you into Himself!

Journey Note

133 *Today's Gem*

We were created for connection. The greatest experience in life is to learn to love and be loved in return. **John 3:16** states, "For God so greatly loved and dearly prized the world that He [even] gave up His only begotten [unique] Son." You see, love gives, and as love gives, it creates a capacity for the giver to receive love in return. That's why the greatest gift we can give each other is love. Not clothes, not toys, not jewelry, but love. Love won't put you in debt. Love won't have you spending money frivolously. So, Sis, give the greatest gift you can—love.

Journey Note

134 *Today's Gem*

Good morning, precious woman of God. The Father wants you to know that you are the apple of His eye. You have no reason to be depressed, oppressed, or discouraged. Things could be so much worse. God wants to remind you that you are pregnant, not only with purpose, but with potential and great possibilities. Okay, so maybe things haven't gone as you've planned, but therein lies the problem. God is orchestrating your process. **Proverbs 16:9** states, "A man's mind plans his way, but the Lord directs his steps and makes them sure." You, woman, are the embodiment of God's expectations. Get your passion back and walk into your promise!

Journey Note

135 *Today's Gem*

Who are you when you take the time to stop being everything to everybody else? Who are you when nobody else is around? You spend your days being wife, mother, sister, daughter, entrepreneur, student, secretary, church member, and friend only to discover that when you are left with yourself, you ask yourself, *"Who am I?" "What do I really want?" "Where do I really want to be?"* Are you vibrant on the outside, yet dying on the inside from silent frustration? Well, it's time for the REAL YOU to come forward. Not the you that is predictable. Not the you that caters to everyone else's needs before your own. But the you that God called to greatness before you were born. The you that is highly favored and blessed among women. If Jesus can call Lazarus from the dead back to life, He can speak life back to your dead dreams, too!

Journey Note

136 *Today's Gem*

Hey, Sis, it's time to make some changes. It's time to stop maintaining what's popular, convenient, and comfortable at the expense of your destiny! I mean, is he really worth it? Sure, he makes you feel good, but at what cost? Is it adding to your walk with God or putting distance there? Or maybe your response to discontentment and disillusionment is doughnuts and candy bars instead of warfare through worship. Stop shortchanging yourself. Today, God imparts courage to you to be the exception. I dare you to be different. You are a piece of artwork. **Ephesians 2:10** says, "For we are His workmanship, recreated and made new in Christ Jesus to do good works which God planned beforehand that we should walk in the good life which He prearranged and made ready for us to live." Be the masterpiece you are!

Journey Note

137 *Today's Gem*

This is dedicated to my dad—Art Kennedy—to Bishop Ralph Dennis (my spiritual dad), and all the other brothers in Christ who push their sisters in Christ to be Every Woman. A godly man is a man who knows who he is, where he is going, and why he is going there. **Hebrews 12:2** declares, "Looking unto Jesus the author and finisher of our faith, who for the joy that was set before Him endured the cross, despising the shame, and is set down at the right hand of the throne of God." Godly men inspire other men. Godly men move nations and command authority as God gives them grace. God is about to release the godly man from the prison of obscurity because you are destined for greatness. You are not what life has dealt you. You are not what your circumstance has labeled you. You are a godly man with power to change a generation. Take your right place—why? So we as women can take ours! Ladies, appreciate the brothers who have protected you along your journey.

Journey Note

138 *Today's Gem*

Genesis 5:2 declares, "He created them male and female and blessed them. And when they were created, he called them 'man.'" Men and women have the same essence but have different designs. God created male and female equal in value but different in function. Man is the head, but he is to rule his household as Christ rules the church—in sacrificial love and in total dependence on God the Father. The issue is male leadership, not male dominance. Healthy male leadership focuses on womanhood expressed, not womanhood suppressed. Purpose determines design. Men and women were designed by God to complement one another. So today, let's celebrate our uniqueness as men and women and know that God designed you for purpose—on purpose.

Journey Note

139 *Today's Gem*

For several years I was a lifeguard and swimming instructor. During the course of ongoing training, I discovered that the deeper and more troubled the water, the harder the rescue was to execute. Those I was privileged and prepared to rescue were always grateful that I was alert and had saved their lives. It wasn't important to me at the time of crisis how they had gotten into that position, I just knew they needed my help. **Galatians 6:1** says, "If a sister is overtaken in misconduct or sin of any sort, you who are spiritual should restore and reinstate her in love and gentleness without any sense of superiority." We are to bear one another's burdens and in this way fulfill and observe the law of Christ. Stay alert—God is calling you to be ready to respond to someone's call for help!

Journey Note

140 *Today's Gem*

Do you have the disease to please? Are you a habitual people pleaser? Oh, you're just nice, right? Well, God wants you to know, Sis, that salvation does not equal doormat and meekness does not equal pushover. Guilt makes you say yes when you really, really want to say no. Why? Because your interpretation of nice is rooted in the desire for approval from others. It's also called insecurity. However, in Christ, you already have God's approval. You are already lovable just as you are, not because of who you are or what you can do, but because of WHO HE IS and WHAT HE HAS ALREADY DONE!

Journey Note

141 *Today's Gem*

It's time for us to become our sister's keeper. In order for us to be a generation of healthy, effective, and productive women, we must avail ourselves of one another. We must begin to build up one another in the spirit of love and rid the Kingdom of the urge to tear each other down. Too often we tear each other down—not by what we do, but by what we don't do. To know a need and not meet it can be just as damaging as inflicting the pain! It's still true—united we stand, divided we fall. **Psalm 133:1** says, "Behold, how good and how pleasant it is for brethren to dwell together in unity." There's power in sisterhood—let's begin to release it!

Journey Note

Our hearts ache because we as women often entrust them to the wrong people. We must keep in mind that our deepest longings can only be satisfied through Christ. Our hearts are sickly because we are emotionally malnourished and spiritually anemic. Spiritual anemia is due to eating improperly—in other words, not absorbing enough of God's Word. This bad habit causes a lack of oxygen-rich blood to travel from our heart to the rest of our body, thereby producing weakness, weariness, and unnecessary worry. **Psalm 62:8** says, "Pour out your heart before Him; God is a refuge for us!" Consume more of God, increase your intake of His Word, and your spiritual deficiency will disappear.

Journey Note

143 Today's Gem

Calling, First Ladies! Yes, you. No, you are not a pastor's wife necessarily. You might not even be married—but you are a lady first. God's elect lady! So honor your own needs; give yourself credit for your accomplishments. Love the little girl within you. Overcome your addiction to approval. Give yourself permission to "play" and enjoy life. Quit being a responsibility sponge—chill out! Feel all of your feelings. It's okay—just act on them appropriately and in a way that pleases God. If you mess up, get up. If you fall down, don't stay down. Nurture others because you want to, not because you have to. Choose what is right and what works for you. Girl, set limits and boundaries and stick to them. Only say yes when you mean it. Have realistic expectations and at the same time unbelievable faith. There's more—tomorrow.

Journey Note

144 Today's Gem

Ladies, anything you have to compromise to get, you never keep. The Lord meets our basic needs for security, significance, and self-worth. Therefore, you don't need to seek approval, affirmation, or acceptance from anyone else. Once Jesus becomes your everything, in Him you live, move, and have your being. In Him, you are blessed with every spiritual blessing. In Him you have redemption, deliverance, and salvation through His blood, the forgiveness of our shortcomings and offenses, in accordance with the riches and the generosity of His gracious favor! Joy Dawson, a wonderful author and speaker, put it this way: "Never minimize the extent of the powerful influence that can come from your life when you make the pursuit of God Himself your complete passion."

Journey Note

145  Today's Gem

One of the biggest reasons people seek relationships with others is because they want intimacy. They want to love and be loved. Sometimes this desire takes people where they don't really want to go. Often in our search for intimacy, we get more than we bargained for and lose more than we realize. But God designed the desire for intimacy to be met in Him. **Proverbs 4:23** tells us, "Above all else, guard your heart, for it is the wellspring of life." God's standards are an umbrella of protection. When we, for whatever reasons, move out from under that umbrella, we no longer benefit from its protection. Desire to live a pure and holy lifestyle. God wants to shift you from devastation to restoration!

Journey Note

146 *Today's Gem*

Are you willing to wait for God's best? **Matthew 6:33–34** says, "But seek and strive after first of all His Kingdom [the place where God rules and reigns] and His righteousness [His way of doing and being right], and then all of these things will be added to your life. So do not worry or be anxious about tomorrow, for tomorrow will have worries of its own. Sufficient for each day is its own trouble and sufficient is our God to handle them." In the meantime, as you pursue the Kingdom of God, and as you pursue the righteousness, holiness, and love of God, you take on the attributes of the one you are pursuing. Thus, you become worthy of God's best. Don't settle for less than what God has for you. You wait on the Lord. You worship the Lord. Simultaneously, He will be adding to your life the desires of your heart. Why? Because your heartbeat has become His and He cannot deny Himself.

Journey Note

147 *Today's Gem*

When helping others is hurting you, its time to let go. You can't manage other people's lives, other people's feelings, other people's priorities—you can only manage yours. Others don't have the power to manipulate how you feel about yourself unless you give it to them. Take your power back and stop dancing to somebody else's song. Girl, write your own song and dance your own dance—freedom looks good on you.

Journey Note

148  *Today's Gem*

Today I want to celebrate my Sister Friends! You know, the girls who make your life as meaningful as it is. In the August 2002 issue of *Ebony* magazine, author Lynn Norment said it this way: "A true Sister Friend is the safety net that keeps you from hitting rock bottom. A true Sister Friend helps you endure the hardships, and get over the failed courtships. When you want to cry, a true Sister Friend will make you laugh out loud. Most importantly, a true Sister Friend will put you in check when the need arises. She tells you the truth — not just what you want to hear. She gives you unconditional love, support, and encouragement just when you need it most." **Proverbs 17:17:** "A friend loveth at all times and a sister is born for adversity." So to all my Sister Friends — I salute you!

Journey Note

149 *Today's Gem*

Girlfriends! How many of us have them? Girlfriends! Ones-you-can-depend-on girlfriends. I'm not talking about the ones who come around when all is well, when the money is flowing, and when the crowd is celebrating you. I'm talking about the ones who stay—when the crowd leaves, your money is funny, and life is dealing you an unfamiliar and strange hand. I'm talking about the ones who speak a "However" when the naysayers say "Never." Girlfriends who admonish you to "Hang in there" when your circumstances are saying, "Girl, give up!" I'm talking about the ones who show up at your house *anyway* when you say don't come. Girlfriends! The ones who stand by you—even when you mess up and let God down. Friends! They don't judge you—they love you back into your rightful place. Girlfriends! The unsung heroes in our everyday lives. Thank you, Girlfriends—you are the wind beneath my wings!

Journey Note

150 *Today's Gem*

It's nice to have friends. But what kind of friend are you? Are you the kind of friend you want to attract? Do you treat your friends the way you want to be treated? **Proverbs 18:24** says, "A woman who has friends must first show herself friendly." Instead of focusing on finding a true friend, focus on *becoming* a true friend. There is a significant difference between knowing someone well and being a true friend. The greatest evidence of genuine friendship is loyalty—showing love at all times. **1 Corinthians 13:7** states, "Love bears up under anything and everything that comes. Love is ready to believe the best of every person and is able to endure anything without weakening." Author Oswald Chambers said it this way: "Once you embrace your encounter with Christ, love is the beginning, love is the middle, and love is the end. After He comes in, all you see is Jesus only—Jesus ever." As Kingdom citizens, we are empowered to love others—not because of who they are, but because of who WE are!

Journey Note

151 *Today's Gem*

What is falling from your tree? What effect do you have on people when you come around? Do you add to or take away from the issue? God is more concerned with you being in the right place than you being in the wrong place doing the right thing. Are you walking in your purpose? **Genesis 1:28** commands us to "be fruitful, multiply, replenish, subdue, and have dominion." Are you manifesting Christ on earth? Well, to know Christ is to know yourself. When you really catch a glimpse of who Jesus is, all that you've done before really doesn't matter anymore. To know Him is to love Him and to love Him is to live (as my friend Minister Veda McCoy would say) — in purpose, on purpose!

Journey Note

152 Today's Gem

I have a message for every woman whose father was absent from her life in one way or another. There is something special about the relationship between a father and his daughter! I believe the father/daughter relationship was designed by God to be a model of the affection God our Father has for each of us. When the father shows up, protection is there. When the father shows up, provision is there. When the father shows up, the priesthood is established and order follows. After order is established, an outpouring is released, which includes affirmation, affection, adoration, and an abundance of love, joy, and peace. Your heavenly Father wants to wrap His arms around you today and cause you to experience the miracle of a father's love. Your life will never be the same!

Journey Note

153 Today's Gem

God the Father loves you right where you are. He wants to hold you. He wants to cover you. He wants to heal you. He wants to fill the voids in your life that cause you to make choices that you later regret. He wants to hold your heart in His hand and protect it from further pain and anguish. God wants to deliver you from that place you never have to see again, and bring you into a place you have never been before. You have been without His direction and guidance long enough. There is something about the confidence and courage a little girl feels when Daddy shows up! She feels she can conquer the world. Where is your father? In spite of where your earthly father may or may not be, what he has or has not done, God said to tell you He's been right there—yeah, right there with you—all the time!

Journey Note

154 Today's Gem

The most wonderful example of a love relationship is **John 3:16**! "For God so loved the world that He gave His only begotten Son." *God gave!* Love gives! If your relationship is taking away from you more than it is giving to you, it is unhealthy. Too often, we as women allow our relationships to jeopardize our emotional well-being for too long, and ultimately end up believing that is the way relationships are supposed to be. Too many women become obsessive in their quest for love, and the root cause is fear. But "God has not given us the spirit of fear, but of power, love and a sound mind." If you have a destructive pattern of relating to others, submit that deficiency to the all-sufficient Christ. He wants to show you what real love is.

Journey Note

155 *Today's Gem*

People are attracted to authenticity. People love people who keep it real, honest, and pure. Stop trying to imitate those who you think have made it and ask God for His blueprint for your life. Who is the real, true, inside you? **Proverbs 14:14** states, "The backslider in heart will be filled with his own ways, but a good man will be satisfied from above." Do you want to be passionately authentic? Then respond to the Word of God with open arms. **Proverbs 16:9** declares, "A man's heart plans his way, but the Lord directs his steps."

Journey Note

156 *Today's Gem*

Seeking God is very similar to developing a friendship. You talk a lot, you listen, you write each other letters, you think about each other, you find out what the other likes and dislikes, and you try to do things that please that person. The more you spend time together, the more intimately you know your friend. And the more intimately you know your friend, the greater your love will be. It works the same way with your relationship with God. **Jeremiah 29:12–13** tells us that when you search for God with your whole heart, you will find Him. When you call, He will listen. Your heart is the key to your devotion to God. You must seek Him with your whole heart. A halfhearted effort is not sufficient—you can't seek God and do your own thing. God wants your whole heart. He wants a pure heart. He wants a listening heart. He is waiting to tell you something about you that amazes you.

Journey Note

157  *Today's Gem*

I want to talk to my single "Sisters in Christ" this morning. Singleness is a gift. The perfect time to make the most of every opportunity is now! You have the ability and the time to develop your love relationship with Christ without distractions that a husband brings to your heart. True love can only be found in undistracted devotion to Jesus Christ. To love Him like this you must know Him intimately, for He is the lover of your soul. Don't limit your search for God to what you can get from Him, such as a man, happiness, or a family! Seek God with your whole heart! Seek God with a pure heart, and do it for who He is, not for what He can do for you.

Journey Note

158 Today's Gem

Many women today are devoted to developing a love relationship—but not with the Lord. They are seeking the world's version of love in sensations, fantasies, and promises. As a woman, God created you with a desire to be known—not just in a physical or general way, but deeply known and intimately loved. If you are hoping a man will one day fill your heart's desire for intimacy, you will be disappointed. Because He is the lover of your soul, only He can fill this need completely. As you come to know who He really is, He will meet your needs for love. God takes delight in His creation and quickly notices every simple effort to please Him. Do you feel like God denies you the things you need most? If you do, then you don't really know Him. Seek Him so you can get to know Him—He is waiting for you.

Journey Note

159 Today's Gem

Anything other than a love relationship with Jesus Christ, regardless of how good that thing may be, will eventually bring you discouragement and disillusionment. Yes, it does satisfy, but only for that moment. The high wears off and then you're left to seek another level of ecstasy. From the time that we're little girls, we are enchanted by fairy tales of the couple living happily ever after. Consequently, we come to believe that marriage is the pinnacle or highlight of life's journey. While it is an exciting chapter in the book of our lives, incompleteness is not the result of being single, but it is the result of not being full of Jesus Christ. Once you abandon your whole heart to Him, you will come to fully understand that you are already complete — in Him!

Journey Note

160 Today's Gem

Are you content to offer to Jesus "that" which costs you nothing? Have you really given Him your whole heart? Or does your relationship with Jesus reflect a superficial effort toward following Him? The answer is found in your honest introspection and review of the level of peace you have with yourself. We were created for intimacy, however, human companionship cannot satisfy the deepest places of the heart. Our hearts are lonely until they find rest in Him. That is why the temporal things you seek **ALWAYS** leave you wanting more. Intimacy with Christ has a high price attached to it. You must give up some things and some people. The depth of your relationship with God is up to you. You can keep what you have or you can get all that rightfully belongs to you. The choice is yours!

Journey Note

161 *Today's Gem*

Hey, Sis, have you fallen in love with Mr. Wrong? Are you the "other woman"? I know you think nobody knows, but God knows, and today He is challenging you to risk having nothing for a moment, so that you can have it all. Yes, the romance is captivating—in the beginning. Eventually, the sweet water will become bitter. The reality is that you are last on the list—in spite of what it looks like. You come after the wife and kids. What you are facilitating is a fantasy, but what you are living is real life! God never intended for you to have crumbs! **Luke 12:32** says, "For it is the Father's good pleasure to give you the Kingdom." Let the love of God help you walk away.

Journey Note

162  Today's Gem

   Are you a woman who loves someone else so much it hurts because you are not getting from them what you feel you need? Well, God wants to change you right now into a woman who loves herself enough to stop the pain! You don't have to earn the right to be happy. You deserve to be happy. If you are more in touch with the dream of how your life could be versus the reality of your situation, God wants to redirect your perspective! Listen, approval and love are two different things. Once you're on the Lord's side, you're approved and loved by Love Himself! Now allow the love of God in you to work through you so love can come out of you and back to you.

Journey Note

163 Today's Gem

A lot of women grew up in families where reality was denied. Secrecy was the rule, not the exception. Consequently, little girls grow into women who lack the ability to relate to people and situations with a healthy sense of reality. You relate out of fear, not love. You fear being alone, being ignored, abandoned, or destroyed. **1 John 4:18** says, "There is no fear in love, but perfect love casts out fear." It's simple . . . If your relationship tank is full of fear, then you need to fill it up with the love of God. How do you do that? Spend some time with the lover of your soul . . . He's been waiting to love you the way you were meant to be loved.

Journey Note

164 *Today's Gem*

A few years ago, Mary J. Blige told the world that she was searching for real love. Many of us become frustrated in our search for love, because although we say we want real love, we often can't find it because we don't know what real love is. Consequently, we often find lust and call it love. Love is patient. Lust is impatient. Love is kind. Lust is unkind. Love considers others. Lust considers its own interests. Love gives. Lust takes until there is nothing left. Love satisfies. Lust leaves you empty. Are you looking for real love that truly satisfies? **Jeremiah 31:3** says that God loves us with an everlasting love. So your search is over not when you discover religion, but when you discover a relationship with Jesus Christ!

Journey Note

 165 *Today's Gem*

I grew up hearing people say, "What you see is what you get." Well, not anymore! Today, what you see is what you get—at that moment. **Lights! Camera! Action!** The devil wants you to go through another day and be something you're not! Resist the temptation to deceive! I'm not talking about the things women do to enhance our outward appearance—those are good things. I'm talking about pretending to be single when you are married! Condemning others for the very thing you struggle with! I'm talking about being her friend and flirting with her husband! **Romans 12:2** tells us to be transformed by the renewing of our mind—let God change the way we think! **Proverbs 23:7** says, "For as a man thinketh in his heart, so is he." So it's not what you see, it's what you think—that's what you get!

Journey Note

Before You Go

$\mathcal{T}$he journey does not stop here, Sis—it simply changes. You have come this far by faith to make it to the next place. John Maxwell said, "In order to be effective and successful, you must become 'growth-oriented' instead of 'goal-oriented.' " Never stop growing because you get so consumed with where you are going. I have learned to enjoy the journey.

I've simply shared the gems I have collected in my treasure chest along MY journey. I pray that at least one of my lessons has lit a fire in you that cannot be extinguished. This light, the glory of God, will guide your feet and light your way to wholeness. Remember, every ending is simply a new beginning. Enjoy the journey to your next place in God. As you go, begin to write your own gems so that those who come along the path you have taken can be empowered by the legacy of your pain, your process, your power, and your promise. May your soul be encouraged to journey on to see what God has in store for you next!